"It is doubtful that anyone has li
Life is filled with trials and suffe
brink of our faith. Carol tells a masterful story that deals honestly with the "whys" of life. Throughout her story, the questions and challenges of a life of faith are portrayed in the life of Jose, an orphaned Mexican boy. But those life challenges and faith trials find meaning when they discover the hope that only comes from the heart of a loving God. This book will encourage all those who find themselves wrestling with the "whys" of life. I couldn't recommend it more!"

—Pastor David Buurma
Valley Community Church
Napa, California

"True-to-life trials pepper the lives of the characters in this tumultuous story of the Southwest. The reader witnesses a young man who discovers one piece at a time of life's perplexing puzzle. Sometimes the protagonist finds only a piece of sky and must set this aside until time reveals the proper connection. Ms. Wilcoxson has threaded this tapestry of a life with the thought that there is no wisdom greater than acts of kindness. Is that not the message that Jesus brought?"

—Barbara Jones
BA—English, Speech, Drama
MS—Adult Education, English
MS—Photojournalism (photography)

No Record of Wrongs reclaims the past of Mexican Americans and Native Indians in a profound and biblical manner. The book reads as a celebration to the miracle of survival of the human spirit. The reader is introduced to amazing folk heroes and various aspects of their cultures, i.e., traditional religious beliefs, language, arts, medicine, relationships, and values. The narratives and adventures move through important historical eras of the twentieth century. The book also makes an important contribution as the reader becomes mindful that the people and their experiences are among the most misrepresented in American history and literature.

—Njoki McElroy, PhD
English professor, Southern
Methodist University, Dallas, Texas
Author of *Natchez 1012*

NO
RECORD
OF
WRONGS

NO
RECORD
OF
WRONGS

A NOVEL

DON OLSON &
CAROL WILCOXSON

TATE PUBLISHING
AND ENTERPRISES, LLC

Published by Tate Publishing & Enterprises, LLC
127 E. Trade Center Terrace | Mustang, Oklahoma 73064 USA
1.888.361.9473 | www.tatepublishing.com

Tate Publishing is committed to excellence in the publishing industry. The company reflects the philosophy established by the founders, based on Psalm 68:11,
"The Lord gave the word and great was the company of those who published it."

Book design copyright © 2012 by Tate Publishing, LLC. All rights reserved.
Cover design by Leah LeFlore
Interior design by Sarah Kirchen

Published in the United States of America

ISBN: 978-1-61862-947-0
1. Fiction / Christian / Historical
2. Fiction / General
12.04.05

This book is dedicated to the memory of my mother, Dorothy Brunson Greene, who taught me not only about God and His love for me but also about how to love others. Her Christian example continues to live in my heart.

—Carol Wilcoxson

ACKNOWLEDGMENTS

I want to thank God for all of His goodness to me and for blessing me with this talent of writing. I hope this book will be used to witness for Him and to honor and glorify him. Thanks be to God!

I would not be a part of this process at all had it not been for my dear friend, Don Olson. He asked me to be his coauthor after many, many hours of our working together on his book. His daughter, Sanna, has continued to provide me with any assistance I have needed.

To Steve Miller, my very dear friend, without whom this book could have never been finished. His digital adeptness has been invaluable to me, since God did not bless me with this gift. Thank you so much, Steve.

And to Karime Jacobo, who works in the literacy section at the Napa, California, Public Library. Karime helped me to be sure all of the research about Mexico was valid.

FOREWORD

For the Methodist reformer John Wesley, when it came to human nature, he was a pessimist, but when it came to God's grace, Wesley was an optimist. In this post-9/11 world, we need more stories of God's grace working in the lives of people who have had, by circumstance and condition, little knowledge of God. Such a story exists in *No Record of Wrongs*.

In this engaging morality story of Jose Chavez, we follow a Mexican goat herder's journey from a real and spiritual orphanage to the creation of a new family and a spiritual adoption. Encountering friends and adversaries along the path to adulthood, Jose meets challenges that refine and guide him from simple superstitions to a simple faith in Jesus Christ. Set primarily in the sparse borderlands of West Texas in the early twentieth century, Jose emerges from this illiteracy of faith to a saving faith. Through Jose's eyes and that of his friends, we are also drawn into the tensions between tightly knit indigenous cultures and an Anglo cowboy culture. In these conflicts of prejudice and ignorance, we see the cynicism of human nature subdued by the redemptive nature of God's grace and justice.

This story is certain to engage young readers and provide teachable moments for parents and grandparents to discuss faith with their children and grandchildren. The story of Jose will entertain and pique a curiosity in the rugged and straightforward manner of the early twentieth-century American Southwest and its people. We are much obliged to Carol and Don for their gift to Christian literature.

—Rev. Dr. Tom Hudspeth
Executive Pastor and Pastor of Deaf Ministries
Lovers Lane United Methodist Church
Dallas, Texas

THE FLOOD

After three days of a monumental downpour, the rain stopped. A small house stood near the Rio Grande River outside of the community of Quemada. Two young goats could be heard bleating. They were hungry today because they had not been able to graze due to the miserable weather. Ten-year-old Jose got up before dawn each day to take them to forage for food on the mountainside nearby.

Hanna, Jose's mother, was already up and had a fire burning between three large rocks on the dirt floor. A clay pot of water was being heated over the flames.

"I have to go to the store to get some charcoal for the fire," she told Jose. "Watch Angelica if she wakes up, and I'll be back soon." Angelica was Jose's little sister.

Because their bellies were empty, the two little goats kept crying. Now they could be seen chewing on the bamboo fence that held them captive. The day before, Angelica had found some dried tortillas and orange peelings along the road to give them. They had licked her little hand, and she had laughed loudly. She was a happy, fun-loving little girl, and Jose loved to play with her.

When Hanna returned, the water was hot and she made the *atole*. This dish was a gruel made out of ground corn, water, stick-cinnamon, and sugar. Every mother in the village would be making *atole* for their family each day about this time. Firelights flickered all over the village this morning, but the blue smoke hovering in each yard made the fires invisible. The homes were all built on sticks and were called, appropriately, stick-houses.

As the women made tortillas, the sound of *pat-pat-pat* could be heard. After taking the pot off the fire, Hanna replaced it with a clay griddle. She started cooking one tortilla while she patted out more, since she always liked to have enough food ready so that she could sit down and eat with her children. After placing the tortillas in a clean cloth bag, she called to Jose, "Please get Angelica up and come to the table for breakfast."

Angelica stirred and then awoke laughing. She got up and immediately walked over to her mother for a morning hug.

"Hi, baby," said Hanna. "I hope you had a good sleep."

Imitating her mother, Angelica took a bit of mashed corn and patted out what looked like a small, thick pancake. Then she looked at Hanna and giggled softly. When it was cooked, she took a stick and moved it to one side where it could cool. In her three-year-old, high-pitched voice, she murmured, "That's for the goats."

After they finished their breakfast, Jose packed a little tortilla lunch for himself in a cloth bag because he needed something to eat while the goats grazed the mountainside.

Jose's dad had left his family to join the army shortly after Angelica was born. Hanna had not heard from him for a long time and the children had finally quit asking about him. He and Hanna had built this house on land no one claimed. They gathered materials from nearby places: bamboo from beside the river, poles from the canyons, and palm from the hillsides. The tiny house was only eight feet long and ten feet wide. A sturdy post was placed at each corner, and crossbeams were tied on the top of each post. These crossbeams provided support for the rafters, which were made of smaller poles. To them were tied straight bamboo poles that reached the full length of the house, plus a little more. Then, using strips of dried palm leaves, Hanna and her husband had connected the bamboo poles four inches apart, all the way up to the rafters. By tying the large palm leaves over everything, the roof became tight and shed any water that might run down when it rained.

The larger poles were bound together with green vines found in the deep canyons. When dry, they formed a secure bond. The door of the house was made of selected bamboo of the same size, and then it was joined together with small cords. At night a rope, tied to one of the posts beside the door, kept the door closed. Jose's house was the last one of a dozen or so like this that had been built along the river.

Quemada was upstream and built on higher ground. Houses here were much more substantial, and many of them were made of adobe brick with tile roofs. It took about fifteen minutes for Jose and his family to walk to Quemada. Once in town, one could see turkeys, chickens, donkeys, and oxen in the courtyards. All Quemadans were farmers who worked in the fields. There were also two stores in Quemada, each of which were located in the corner room of a private home. Both stores carried a few items like corn, flour, sugar, thread, soap, charcoal, matches, candles, and candy.

Quemadans were all of Mexican descent. In the village was a small graveyard adjacent to a Catholic church. Having cracked walls and falling plaster, the church needed a lot of repairs. Peeling wax and paraffin covered the altar, and images of the saints were covered with dust and in need of new clothing and face paint. Other icons were simply pushed together into a dark corner. A priest visited Quemada once a month.

From the steps of the church you could see the river clearly as it crashed through the rocks, making a noise like a high water-fall. The force of the water as it rushed full speed toward lower ground sounded like a booming canon.

Jose decided that he needed to go ahead and leave the house if he were to get the goats some food. He took his old, broken machete and put his cloth bag over his shoulder. As he hugged his mother, she said, "May the blessed Virgin be kind to you today."

Angelica was looking and listening intently. Jose hugged her tightly, and she clung to him. Breaking away gently from her, he said, "Now you be sure you help our mother today." He opened the goat pen and grabbed the two ropes that were around the necks of the animals. He tied the ropes together so that one goat couldn't get far without the other. Knowing exactly which way to go, the goats trotted away.

The sky was blue and clear, and Jose was expecting a pleasant day. However, there was an oppressive feeling in the air, and he attributed it to the rains that had saturated the ground. The goats stopped frequently to nibble on tufts of grass near the trail.

When they finally arrived where there was plenty to eat, Jose looked for firewood. Usually he found enough sticks to take home. The terrain was rocky, and cacti were everywhere. As he searched for sticks, he had to watch out for the many snakes that were all around. He enjoyed the solitude that was his while he fed the goats. He could see other herders some distance away, but he seldom talked to anyone.

The goats, bleating only occasionally, ate their fill. The sun shone brightly overhead, and Jose observed his shadow as only a sliver of shade near his feet. Becoming hungry, he tied the goats to a nearby shade tree and sat on a rock to eat. Looking up into the sky once again, he saw black clouds forming in the distance. The goats became eager to be untied, so he took them to a place where they could drink water. He too drank from the cool stream coming out of the hillside.

Suddenly, a violent whirlwind ripped by. As if it were a live beast, it tore at the bushes and trees around him. Jose became frightened, and he felt even more threatened as the black clouds came closer and closer. Now he wondered if he should just turn around and go back home. Loud claps of thunder could be heard in the distance. Everything around him stopped, and an eerie silence prevailed. It was as if the world had come to a screeching halt.

As the sounds of thunder came nearer, he began to see flashes of lightning crashing around him. Big drops of rain splattered everywhere, and the wind was so strong that it blew Jose and the goats from one place to another. They could no longer stand up, and Jose was freezing. The trio finally found a spot protected from the wind. Tugging at the ropes, the goats led Jose to a large, overhanging rock, where there was a little shelter.

The torrential downpour and cold wind drove the saturated air in all directions. As the skies became darker, Jose could see nothing but rain. Hours passed, and he had no idea what time it was.

The goats lay down contentedly with no worries in the world. However, Jose thought that there might be wild animals around, and he was the only one who could defend himself against them. For a long time, he sat between the two goats and felt the warmth from their bodies. Wondering about his mother and Angelica, he prayed, *O Virgin, keep them safe.*

Remembering how tightly Angelica had hugged him and what his mother had said to him helped to calm him down. Finally, he slept. The long night passed, and the rain stopped.

At daybreak, the goats stood up and were ready to eat again, but Jose forced them to go toward the village. The washed ground no longer looked the same as it had the day before, and he couldn't locate the bundle of sticks he had collected. No matter. He had to hurry home now.

As he drew near the village, he saw many people milling about. They seemed to all be talking loudly and shouting, sometimes to everyone and sometimes to no one in particular. Concern was written on every face. The church bell rang loudly, heralding some important message. Jose didn't even stop to find out what all the excitement was about but tugged on the ropes and urged the goats to hurry.

Up ahead, he could see the vast spread of water over areas of land that were always dry. None of the houses that stood by the river were still there. Water and debris clung to bushes and trees; parts of houses, trees, and dead animals floated by. At last Jose located two of the corner posts that had once been a part of his home. There was nothing else left. The posts stood as mute witnesses in the midst of a vast lake of water, mud, and sand. He stood there unbelieving, bewildered, and wondering what to do.

"Did you live here? Last night a six-foot-tall wall of mud and water smashed into all of the houses that were here, and they were carried away." A big man had come up behind Jose and spoken.

"I wonder what happened to my mother and little sister," said Jose. "Do you know where they are? It rained very hard last night, and they would not have left in the rain."

"Come with me to the village and we will search for them," the man said. "Maybe one of the neighbors has seen them."

"And if not?" Jose left the question dangling as he took the rope that held the goats nearby.

Returning to the village, they mingled with the crowd. Jose was famished since he had had nothing to eat for almost twenty-four hours, but he had no money to buy food. He spotted a woman who had once bought tortillas from his mother and she too was selling them.

He approached her. "Have you seen my mother and little sister?"

She answered negatively, and he asked another woman, "Have you seen Hanna Chavez?"

"No, and she used to come here every day. Where are she and that darling little girl of hers?"

"Who are you?" another woman inquired.

"I am Jose, Hanna's son," replied Jose.

All of the women then began to wonder if Hanna and Angelica had survived the flood.

Jose continued. "I just don't know where my family could be. Our house is gone, and nothing is left of where we once lived."

"You poor boy," one woman exclaimed, "I'll bet you must be hungry. Have these tortillas now."

"Thank you," said Jose, gulping them down.

"Maybe your mother is staying with friends or has gone to Big Town," the woman added in an attempt to keep hope alive in the child.

Jose surprised even himself by voicing his own thoughts to these strangers. "They are dead."

Big tears started running down his cheeks. He knew in his heart that they were gone and would never be back. Becoming overwhelmed by this thought, he took the goats and went to the back of the church. Crying uncontrollably, alone and afraid, he sobbed until there were no more tears left. Then he wiped his face on his sleeve, leaving his cheeks smudged with dirt.

After purging himself of his tears, he began to stare into space. He thought about how the huge waves of mud and water must have looked as they swept all of the houses away.

He said, "God, if you are here, why did you allow this to happen?"

Little did he realize that this question would haunt him for many years to come. Jose knew little about this God who had created all things. He remembered one time, though, when he was younger that he and his dad had been lying on a quilt together outside looking at the stars. He had asked his dad, "Who made all these stars, and what keeps them from falling out of the sky?"

His father had answered as best he could. "God created them all, and He holds them in his hand."

Jose even remembered how the stars had looked that night and thought of the sky as a dark blue quilt that contained some of God's most beautiful creations.

His reverie came to a quick end as he heard a woman's voice. Her name was Paula, and the vendors had told her where to find Jose. She lived in a nearby hacienda along with her husband, Ramon, who rarely was seen in town. They were known to the other villagers as people who had money for whatever they wanted. They had no children of their own but nearly always had a boy or a girl in the house to do errands and simple chores.

Paula knelt down beside Jose and put her arm around him. Holding him close for a moment, she said, "Come home with me. You can stay with us. I know your mother and sister, so tomorrow, or whenever the water goes down, we can go look for them."

Jose replied, "I have to take these goats to the fields so they can eat."

"We have food for them at home. Come now. I'll show you where you can stay as long as you like."

They walked to the edge of town, and Jose noticed an old ranch house ahead of them. The walls were cracked and in disrepair. Termites had riddled the huge wooden doors. A long pole, extending above the top of the wall, was part of a plow that farmers used to break up the soil. Paula opened a small door, which was built into one half of a larger door. When they were inside, she slid the board-lock in place to keep the door closed. The yard was neat, but it showed signs of chickens and turkeys that roamed freely. The adobe walls were thick, but light came through huge cracks from where much of the white plaster had fallen.

They stepped into the corridor, a porch-like structure that was a catchall for about everything they owned. It served as a place to visit or to conduct business. Another wooden door led to a large bedroom, which was dark inside because there were no windows. However, the open door let some light in. Jose saw a long wooden table with a few chairs around it. Palm mats, rolled up in the corner, were used for sleeping. A blanket or two were folded and stacked on the table. One more item in the room caught Jose's eye: a large box with four legs and a cover that folded down. It was called a *baul*. Valuables were kept in it, along with important papers, pictures, and money. Several old calendars and pictures of Mexican presidents hung on the walls of the room.

Paula stirred up the coals from the morning fire and added some dry wood. The fire was a welcome sight, and she put a pot of *atole* over it; Jose quickly drank a bowlful, and Paula gave him another.

"Don't go to the fields today," she told him. "I have fodder to feed your goats."

Then Paula took him to the backyard where the animals stayed. There were short posts stuck in the ground where the oxen were tied when they were home. And a donkey stood in the sunlight, fighting flies that lit on its back. Paula brought a bundle of corn stalks with dried leaves and put them down for the goats. Chickens and turkeys wandered around, pecking at things to eat: a green blade of grass, a leaf, or a bug. Jose sat on a low stool while he watched the fire burn.

Paula asked Jose, "Where were you when the flood came?"

"I was out on the mountainside. I watched as the storm came nearer and nearer, but I thought it would be over soon. So I didn't go back home. The wind grew stronger, and the goats pulled me in the direction of some rocks where we found a little shelter. At least we were able to keep dry. The sky became black and I couldn't see anything, so I spent the night there and came home as soon as I could. When I got here, I saw that my house had been washed away by the flood." He could hardly bring himself to admit the truth that he sensed in his heart.

Paula, with great compassion in her voice, said, "Your mother and sister are gone." Tenderly, she continued. "They are all right. Don't worry about them. They know you are hurting inside, and they are sorry you have to go through this grief and pain. But they are happy now, and they are feeling no pain or sadness.

Her words, meant to be of comfort, were beyond a ten-year-old boy's understanding. Jose wanted to believe what Paula had told him, but he was not sure.

"How do you know that they are okay?" Jose asked. "Has anyone been where they are now?"

Paula could see that he wasn't joking or making fun of her belief that his family was now fine. He possessed a child's sincerity and faith.

"They teach this at church," Paula replied. "Someday you will understand this for yourself. Have you been baptized?"

"I don't know. My mother didn't tell me. What is it?"

"Some weeks after a baby is born, his parents take him to church. There, a priest dips his finger in water and places it on the baby's head. The priest says, 'In the name of the Father, Son, and Holy Ghost.' That's all there is to it."

"And what if the baby isn't—what did you say—baptized?"

Paula didn't want to reply, and Jose sensed her reluctance.

Somewhat warily, he spoke up. "I'm sure Angelica was not baptized. My mother spoke of it but never did it. So where is she?"

"They say she's in a place called 'Limbo.' It's like sleeping. She isn't suffering or anything. Her soul is waiting there for people to pray for her. Then she will join your mother in heaven."

This subject was getting beyond Paula's ability to comprehend, much less explain to a child. "Let me show you where you can sleep," she said as she led him to a corner, set apart by a hanging palm mat. "Maybe you want to take a nap now. You must be tired. When my man gets home this evening, we'll have soup and tortillas to eat."

Jose lay down and soon fell fast asleep. He dreamt of his mother and Angelica. They were happy and seemed just as real as if they were still alive. Suddenly, he awoke to the sound of a man's voice yelling at the oxen. Oxen move at their own, slow pace, no matter what is said or how loudly it is spoken. Jose sat up and watched the man disengage the yoke from their necks. Long bands of leather were wound around the yoke and the horns of each animal. Made of a single log, the yoke was carefully carved out so that it would exactly fit the oxen's necks. The man put a small rope through the ring in each of the ox's noses, and then he led them to drink from a tank of water. After tying each to its own stake, he threw corn leaves in front of them. Jose watched and waited in silence until the man sat down at the table.

Noticing Jose, the man asked gruffly, "Who are you, and what are you doing here?" It was Ramon, Paula's husband. Paula then answered, "This is Jose, Ramon, and he lost everything in the flood, including his mother and little sister. I brought him here until he can find another place to stay."

This seemed to satisfy Ramon, who immediately saw in the boy someone who could work for his keep. In the future he would get Jose to help him work in his fields.

"Those two goats out in the pen, whose are they?"

"They are mine," Jose answered politely. "I'll take care of them and take them out to eat on the mountain."

They ate supper in silence, and when they had finished, Ramon got up and went outside to smoke. He rolled some tobacco in a husk of corn, twisted the end so that the tobacco wouldn't fall out, and lit up. The smell was sweet. He smoked another and yet another.

Ramon was a frugal man, wasting nothing. Having led a life of austerity, he was "all business" and had only two goals for himself: to accumulate land and plant more corn. Paula, on the other hand, was fun loving. She enjoyed chatting with people and spending money for little things, which brought her pleasure.

The next morning at dawn Jose, who had been crying in his sleep, awakened to a loud noise.

"Young man, get up and help me with the water. Take a pail with a rope on it and fill up the tank from the cistern."

Jose did as he was told. After that, the man ordered him to go to the well some distance away and bring a clay pot full of clean water for drinking. Again Jose obeyed, feeling that he should work for the food he ate.

Paula gave them *atole* and tortillas. Ramon then left with his oxen yoked together. They carried the plow on top of the yoke between them while the end of the pole dragged on the ground.

"I'm leaving too," said Jose. "I'll be back this afternoon."

Paula put some tortillas into a clean cloth and dropped them into Jose's bag. He picked up his old machete and led the goats out on the street. The path led past the church, where people were still gathering to talk about all of the awful damage that the flood had caused. Jose learned that some men planned to go down to the river to see if any bodies could be found, and if so, they would be brought back to the village for burial. Jose decided to join them.

He went ahead of the search party. About a mile from the village, he tied the goats in a little patch of grass. Then he began searching for anything that might be useful in identifying some-one who had lost his or her life. Moving a small log, he saw a corner of a leather object sticking out of the mud. He pulled on it and found a leather billfold. After brushing it off and open-ing it up, he saw some water-soaked papers and eight dollars. Quickly, he put the billfold in his pocket because he decided that he could use the money. Jose started crying again when he thought about what had happened to the person who had once owned the billfold.

The men from the village were searching another area not far away. As Jose watched, one of the men pulled a child's shoe from the sand. He put it in his shoulder bag to show later to those looking for loved ones. An observer could tell that, although it had receded by now, water had risen to the height of almost six feet above normal. There were bits of clothing, dead branches, garbage, and dried bamboo leaves clinging to many of the trees and bushes. Many animals had died.

A little farther on, Jose saw a rag doll partially buried. He pulled it free and then hastily threw it away. It reminded him of Angelica. He just couldn't stand the thought that she might have been cast aside by the fury of the muddy water and, like the doll, lay lifeless and far away from anyone who had cared for her.

Looking toward the south, Jose could see many small lakes on both sides of the river. There was no way the men could cover all of that vast area in search of the dead.

When Jose returned to the search party, one of the men said to him, "You know, son, that it's useless to search anymore."

Jose found his goats and moved them to another spot. Then he kept on looking. He came to a clump of roots from a bamboo cluster that had settled in the sand. Walking around it, he searched carefully for something of value. There, almost hidden by leaves, was an arm sticking out of the mud. Jose couldn't tell if it belonged to a man or a woman. He couldn't possibly remove the body, so he piled some debris over it. He looked around for a stable landmark so he could find his way back. Spotting a big tree branch nearby, he decided it would not move until he could return with help.

When he got back to the church, the men were talking about their fruitless search. The man who found the shoe pulled it from his bag and showed it to the others who were there. Jose saw that no one recognized the shoe, so he drew closer and examined it.

"This shoe belonged to my little sister," he said sadly. He kept it—it was the only tangible evidence that she had been in the flood. He didn't know if he should tell the men about the arm he had seen in the sand. Would anyone believe him? He looked around at the other men and saw only one who had shown concern on his face when Jose had claimed his sister's shoe. Jose motioned for the man to come to one side.

"I stayed back after the men left," he said in a low voice. "I came across an arm sticking out of the mud. The body was covered, so I don't know if it is a man or a woman."

"What did you do?" the man asked.

"I covered it over with leaves and grass and put rocks over it."

The man told the mayor of the town, since he would be able to decide what to do. He was responsible for reporting any deaths to the authorities in Big Town. After hearing the man's story, the mayor chose four men to go on a search for bodies again the next morning.

Approaching Jose, he asked, "Do you think you can find that place tomorrow?"

"Sure," said Jose. "It has to be someone who got swept away in the storm, and I know I wouldn't forget how to get there."

Soon nearly everyone in town knew a body had been found, and they were anxious to find out whose it was. Paula, not wishing to miss out on a thing, was nearby, chatting with the other women. Jose spotted her, and they went home together.

The next morning, the four men took shovels, a stretcher made of gunnysacks, and some formaldehyde that they would use to stifle the awful smell of death. Jose went with them, but he had a hard time keeping up. No one said much of anything as he led them to the spot. He removed the rocks he had placed over the body, and the men quickly removed the tree limb and other debris.

"Well, he was right!" one of the men exclaimed. "Now how will we go about this?"

The self-appointed leader looked things over. "Dig beside the body until the hole is deep, but we will have to be careful that the loose sand, branches, and tough bamboo leaves don't get in the way."

After the mud was removed, a man's body was found. The men covered the body with a cloth made of old flour sacks. Then a crude cross was made with sticks nearby, and this was stuck in the mud. Two men picked up the stretcher, and everybody began a somber walk back to the village.

Every few minutes the men exchanged places with each other.

As they hurriedly approached the edge of the village, people could be seen waiting for them. They stood watching and wondering whose body this could be. Some made the sign of the cross. An even larger crowd gathered near the church. They looked aghast as the body was let down to the ground and the cloth was removed.

"Do any of you know who this man is?" the mayor asked them all. When no one responded, he asked if the body had any kind of identification on it. One of the men felt into the pockets of the man's clothes, but he could find nothing. Upon lifting the collar of the man's shirt, he spotted a small gold chain around his neck. After removing the chain, the man gave it to the mayor, who held it up and showed it to the crowd.

One man came forward. "This man looks like he could be somebody I've seen in Big Town."

"Take the body to the churchyard and put it under a shade tree," the mayor ordered. "If nobody claims it by tonight, we'll go ahead and bury it here.

During all of this time, Jose was listening and observing. He could hardly believe that the dead man would never walk or talk again.

"Come home with me," said the man whom Jose had first told about his discovery. "You look like you could use some clean clothes after all you have done. My son is grown up now, but I think we still have some of his clothes at home. They're still good and will probably fit you just fine. My name is Vicente."

After Jose bathed and voiced his thanks to Vicente and his wife for their hospitality, he picked up his old clothing to leave.

Vicente said to him, "If you ever need anything else, please feel free to ask us."

On the way home, Jose's curiosity got the best of him, and he went by the church again to see what was happening.

JOSE AND PAULA

The news of a body having been found had spread far and wide. All the people of the town were gathering together near the body, and a middle-aged woman was looking at it carefully. Finally, she told the mayor that it was her husband.

"Did he carry any identification?" the mayor asked.

"He usually had a gold chain around his neck," replied the woman.

Pulling the chain with the little cross out of his pocket, the mayor inquired of her, "Is this it?"

She held it close to her eyes and nodded. "Yes, I'm sure it's his. I want to get a casket and give him a proper burial. Will you give me permission to bury him in the churchyard?" she asked timidly.

The mayor nodded and the people dispersed. They were glad that the body had been claimed. The woman needed money quickly for a casket and for somebody to dig the grave. She knew of only one person in Quemada who might lend her money. So she asked where Ramon lived.

The mayor replied, "This boy here can take you to his house." He pointed to Jose.

When she and Jose arrived at the door, he announced his arrival, and they entered the house together. Ramon was home, but he seemed grumpier than usual. The field he had been working in that day had been washed with the heavy rains, and much of the good soil was gone. He wanted to plant corn, but the land was too wet to plow. If he waited much longer to plant, the phase of the moon would not be right. That could cause the crop to be poor and full of bugs.

Ramon and the woman talked a bit about the flood and the damage it had done. She soon got right to the point. "You heard about the men who found a body buried in the river south of here, right? It was my husband's, and he is now lying in the churchyard. I need some money to buy a casket and bury him. Would you do me the great favor of lending me twenty dollars?"

"What have you got to pay me back?" Ramon asked.

"I have some chickens and a pig. I'll take them to market on Sunday and pay you back right away."

Ramon had heard many similar promises that were never kept, and he saw a chance to make some money. "You will have to pay me twenty dollars more than the loan."

He went into his bedroom, opened the big box, and took out the money. The arrangement was not unusual. Lenders, even banks, charged 10 percent per month interest on loans. It was not just the rich exploiting the poor but the poor exploiting the poor when they could. The woman wrapped the money in a wrinkled red handkerchief and put it in her bosom. Jose felt deep compassion for her and came close to giving her the eight dollars he had found, but she left hurriedly.

Paula knew that she should explain to Ramon that Jose had taken the men to the river and that he had not taken the goats out to graze.

"I don't know why you brought that boy here," Ramon said angrily. "The goats are eating up my fodder, and with the heavy rains, there will be a shortage next year."

"Be generous," Paula retorted. "I'll pay for the cornstalks those goats eat."

When angry, Ramon often beat an ox or the donkey with a leather belt or an ox goad. He yelled at them for little or no reason. When a hungry person came to the door, he would turn him away, saying, "You should work for what you need." Paula would always give away food, like eggs or bread. She had her own income from raising chickens and turkeys. The only thing she asked of Ramon was the corn with which to make his tortillas. She often thought that his attitude was bad because his first wife had died and left him with a daughter, Corazon, who was ten years old. Ramon's sister had raised Corazon, and now she was grown and worked in San Antonio. Occasionally, Corazon would visit Ramon at Christmastime.

Paula had wanted to be married by a priest in the Catholic Church, but Ramon would not hear of it—they were married by a justice of the peace in a one-ring ceremony. Paula had never taken the ring off of her finger. After the wedding, a few neighbors gave them a party. One person gave them a pig, another one gave two chickens, and a third one gave a grinding stone. Others brought cooking utensils as their gift. Everything, including the approximate price of the objects, was noted in a book. This same thing was done when somebody passed away and people came to the wake. If they brought candles or soft drinks, everything was carefully written down. Then, when the giving party had a family function, such as a wedding or a funeral, you were to repay in kind. It would not be right to owe for gifts you had once received.

At last Jose took his two goats to the hillside to graze. He looked for firewood, made a bundle of sticks, and brought them home. Then he dropped them on the floor near the fire. Paula looked pleased and soon invited Ramon and Jose to eat. She served them a soup with big pieces of chicken in it. Jose had never tasted such delicious food, and he told her so.

"My mother never put meat in soup," he said. "We always ate tortillas and *atole*, and then the next meal was the same thing."

Paula laughed at this. Ramon pushed himself from the table and prepared his smokes while Paula and Jose chatted about the events of the day.

"Let's go back to the church to see what's going on," he suggested.

Ramon left the room and the two of them sat in silence. Jose was pensive, and Paula noticed his sad face.

"Are you thinking about your mother and sister?" she asked.

"Yes," he replied. "I'm still feeling sad about what happened to them. And where was God in all of this?"

"I don't know," responded Paula.

"When I was down by the river, I found a wallet with money in it. What shall I do with it?"

"We'll try to find out who it belongs to. Were there any papers or cards in it?" she asked.

"Yes," replied Jose. "Here are the papers I found in the wallet."

Neither Paula nor Jose could read the words written on the papers. It was then that she realized that Jose had not been to school and that he couldn't read.

"If we can't find out whose wallet this is, the money belongs to you," she assured him.

He put the things back into his cloth bag, and together they went out into the darkness. She was glad to have some company and would have never gone out alone by herself at that time of night.

They arrived at church and saw that the body was lying in a cheap wooden casket. Candles were burning brightly on the altar. The man who dug the grave was waiting for his pay, and the widow gave him some coins. Jose was eager to find the owner of the billfold, and he gave it to Paula.

They approached a group of men talking softly among themselves. She greeted them. "Can you read a name on any of these papers?"

Those who could read examined them, but came up with no answer. Others, seeing what was happening, drew near the group and looked on. Someone asked, "Where did you get these?"

Paula answered discreetly, "They were found in the mud after the flood."

There was little point in staying longer since the burial would be early in the morning. The odor of formaldehyde mixed with camphor was strong, and Jose wanted to get away.

He asked Paula, "Could I come back in the morning? I want to see how things are done in preparing for the funeral."

He just wanted to understand how the body would be prepared. He thought about his own mother and little sister. If their bodies were ever found, he would know something about the burial process.

The next morning, after having a meager breakfast, Paula and Jose arrived at the graveyard beside the church, where a priest was beginning a short mass. When it was over he asked, "Has the dead man ever been baptized?"

"I don't know," replied the widow woman.

"Then I will have to baptize him," the priest said in a mechanical manner. After opening the casket, he lifted a corner of the cloth that covered the man's face. Taking a small bottle of water out of his pocket, he placed his finger in it and touched the man's forehead. He placed a crucifix on his chest and intoned, "He is now with Jesus."

Jose wondered what this was all about. He didn't understand the ritual that was taking place.

After the widow paid the priest and thanked him for coming, the casket was lowered to the grave. Jose observed two ropes being placed under it, one on each end. There was sufficient length of rope on both sides to reach down to the bottom of the hole. With one man on each end of the rope, they slowly lowered the casket to the bottom. Being careful to see that the man's head was facing northward, they removed the ropes, and immediately people began to shovel dirt into the hole. Dull sounds of dirt and rocks falling on the boards made Jose sad. While the men were filling the hole, the widow lady threw in the dead man's clothes and shoes, one by one. Soon the hole was filled, and a small mound of dirt marked the grave. In time the dirt would settle and the ground would remain more or less level. A weather-beaten cross was found nearby and placed on the mound.

Paula and Jose returned home, and she reminded herself that it was Saturday. On Sunday, they would be going to Big Town to do some shopping. The town was ten miles away, and, like many women and children, Paula and Jose would walk. Ramon, being the man of the house, got to ride his donkey. Jose's excitement mounted as he thought of going into town. He had never been to Big Town.

The next morning, after the animals had been watered and fed, Jose asked, "Can we leave now? I have my money with me, and I really want to go."

Paula smiled at him and said, "Of course. We don't want to miss anything."

Meanwhile, Ramon was putting a thick cushion on the sleepy donkey's back and cinching the cushion tightly around him. Then he started off toward town. Many other people were on the road too, and many of them were barefoot. The bottoms of their feet were well-calloused by walking around with no shoes most of the time. Because of this, they had no problem walking over stones and thorns.

As they approached Big Town, everyone could hear the buyers and sellers yelling back and forth to each other. Oxen, yoked together, were paraded in front of a potential buyer. Docile older animals, used to the plow or oxcart, never gave any trouble to whomever was prodding them to move along. However, the younger animals often gave problems. They would refuse to obey the owner's yells and ox goads. Buyers would often buy calves and yearlings and take them home until they grew larger and were ready for slaughter. Butchers from near and far also came to the market. Often, they would ask the seller, "Where did this animal come from?" In a tired voice, a seller would reply, "From a great distance down the road. This trip caused me considerable work, and I am worn out. I am not anxious to take this animal back home." Then the buyer and seller would haggle over the price to be paid for the animal. The buyer would always win, so the seller would end up selling it for considerably less than it was worth.

The horses caught Jose's attention. Paula had a hard time getting him to leave them. He admired the riders who put their horse through its paces. Looking at every horse carefully, he dreamed of the day when he could have a horse of his own.

Continuing farther into town, Paula and Jose saw the merchants putting out their wares on the roadway. Some put up shades made of flour sacks sewn together that were supported by bamboo poles. They sold almost everything that was needed for rural living: corn, both for eating and for planting; potatoes and beans; plow shares; machetes; leather goods and clothing; dishes and cheap cooking utensils; and much more.

Paula and Jose browsed for a while and looked around at everything. Arriving at a booth where dozens of sandals were displayed, Jose picked up a pair.

Paula looked at them. "You see how these sandals have very thin soles and thin straps? Let's see if we can find a pair that are well made and of good leather. The sandals that you are holding are made of plastic and will soon come apart." She put them down. "You pick out a pair that you like and that are made like the ones I just told you about."

After trying on several pair, Jose picked up a pair of light brown leather sandals. "I like these a whole lot, and they feel really comfortable. May I have them?"

Paula did not reply but looked at the seller standing next to her and said, "How much are these?

"They are a dollar and nine cents," the man replied.

Paula gasped audibly, showing her unbelief and displeasure. "I'll give you seventy-nine cents for them."

"No way," the man exclaimed. "They are worth what I ask, but since you are my first customer, I'll sell them to you for ninety-nine cents."

After offering him eighty-nine cents, Paula started to walk toward the next booth.

Seeing that she was looking at the merchandise elsewhere, the man took the sandals over to her. "You may have them."

Taking his money out of his pocket, Jose handed him a five-dollar bill. Jose showed the change to Paula, and she looked at it and remarked, "That's correct."

Moving on, they soon came to hats of all types that were stacked on the road. These were cheap palm hats that nearly all the country folks wore. On a table nearby were a few expensive broad-brimmed hats of various colors. Picking out a palm hat for boys, Paula put it on Jose's head. Then she retied the one string inside it so that it would fit Jose's head.

"You need to wear a hat outside in the sun," she advised.

Jose gave the seller twenty cents.

Paula told Jose, "Now I am going to buy some bread and cocoa beans. We will soon have a celebration, and I will save them for that occasion." This statement had little meaning for Jose since he had never eaten bread or tasted chocolate.

Cocoa beans were as good as cash. People would trade eggs, beans, or corn for them. Toasted on a griddle and then ground up and mixed with sugar, the beans were made into a chocolate drink. Chocolate was becoming more and more popular with people, and cocoa became the preferred treat for special occasions. Not many years before, four beans were of the same value as an old Spanish coin called a *tlaco*. Sometimes the *tlaco* was cut in halves or fourths to buy items of less value.

After buying four or five handfuls of the brown beans, Paula walked on. She passed a stand that was selling charcoal, but she decided that she didn't need any. After she bought bread from somebody she knew, they were ready to return home.

"Wait," Jose said. "I would like to buy a sharp knife. I saw some over there." He pointed to a store.

The two ambled over to the store and went inside.

"Can you help me with a knife?" Jose said.

The man showed them a few knives, and Paula kept insisting on buying a knife that was made of good steel.

Reaching into a drawer, the man pulled out two knives. "These are not cheap," he said.

"How much?" asked Jose as he searched for the rest of his money.

Picking up one of the knives with two blades, the man said, "This one is a dollar and a half."

Jose looked at Paula, and she knew he would be terribly disappointed if they went home without that knife. So he paid for it and carefully put it in his back pocket. Paula bought a notebook and two pencils.

The long walk home was hot and tiring. As they approached the door, Jose exclaimed joyfully, "Thank you, Paula. This has been a great day."

Jose took the goats to the field, and he pulled up some edible weeds that they could nibble after they got home. It looked like rain in the western sky, so he stayed close to the village.

When he got home, Ramon was there. He had bought two large baskets made of bamboo. He also found three small orphaned goats that were bleating pitifully for their mothers.

"Now you have five goats to care for," he told Jose.

Jose saw that one kid was all black; another was brown with a white face and brown legs; and the third one was mottled with colors of black, gray, and white. He did not know how he would handle three small goats. They were frail, delicate, and still needing to nurse. Confined to a small pen, they showed no interest in anything. They just stood there, bewildered and crying for their mother, just as Jose had cried for his.

SCHOOL

The next morning, Jose awoke to the loud bleating of the goats. After getting up, he wondered what he could find to feed the little ones. He didn't want to take them to the fields because he knew they couldn't eat solid food yet.

Ramon was gone, having taken the oxen out to the fields to graze. Paula had made the *atole* and also had the tortillas ready.

She said to Jose, "I bought some cow's milk this morning to see if we could get the little goats to drink it. I also have some alfalfa here, and maybe they will eat these green leaves." Paula warmed the milk slightly and placed it before one of the small goats. It smelled the milk and turned away.

"How are we going to get it to drink?" Jose asked.

Putting a small amount of milk into a chamois bag, Paula tilted the goat's head back and poured the milk into its mouth.

The milk went down, so she did it again. The other two goats got the same treatment, but it seemed harder for them to drink easily, perhaps because they were so little.

"They'll get used to it in time," she said confidently. "Now let's see if they want to eat any alfalfa."

They didn't, so she took a bit of mashed corn and put it in a shallow clay dish. That didn't work either, but at least they had a bit of milk inside their bellies. Like abandoned babies, the goats kept bleating and crying for their mother's milk. Jose felt sorry for them and he wondered if they would really survive.

"I'll take one of the little ones with me. I can't handle them all!" he told Paula.

Jose took the sturdiest of the three, but it had never been tied to a rope. Jose's goats, resenting the baby goat, pulled on the ropes and wanted to get out to where they could eat the grass. His goats butted the smaller goat whenever they could. Finally, Jose picked it up and carried it. When they reached a patch of grass, he stopped and let the goats forage for whatever they could find. Bits of grass, leaves, and cactus plants filled the goats' stomachs before long. The young goat looked scared and bewildered.

That evening, Paula, taking some mashed corn left over from breakfast, made a marble-sized ball and put it far down in the goat's throat. It went down, so she did it two more times. After doing the same thing with the other two goats, she let them loose in the pen. The next day, they went through the same routine again—a little milk and some of the corn dough.

"I believe they are going to live," exclaimed Jose to Paula. "I saw one of them nibbling on some green leaves today."

"Yes, they'll make it," Paula replied. "Soon you will be able to take them all to the field since they are getting bigger."

As the summer days passed by and fall drew near, Paula spoke to Jose about going to school. At the age of ten, he could not read.

Ramon objected. "And who will take care of the goats? He has to earn his keep."

Paula, though, had it all figured out. "Ramon," she said. "Jose can take the goats to the fields for a couple of hours before school each day and again in the afternoon."

Only a few children went to school, and there was only one teacher for all six grades. The one-room schoolhouse was close to the center of town. This year the town had hired a new bilingual teacher for the school. His name was Mr. Abeda, and he was a graduate of the teacher's training school nearby.

Classes started on the first day of September and ended on the last day of May each year. The children got out during December for two weeks and one week in May around Easter. Because many girls didn't attend school, there were more boys than girls. For recreation, there were swings and an open space where all could have a good time and enjoy themselves. Most of the time they had no ball to play with, so they would kick a tin can or a wad of rags rolled up tightly and tied.

Upon arriving at school on the first day, Jose was asked by Mr. Abeda to write his name in a book.

"I can't read or write, sir," Jose replied.

"So," said the teacher, "you will be in first grade, along with two others."

Jose felt embarrassed and the other students snickered. Looking down at the floor, he wished he hadn't come.

The open fields and clean air are better than this closed, stuffy room, he thought.

After Mr. Abeda looked over the names of all of the students, he placed them in the proper classes. One of the girls in the first grade was named Ruth, but most of the students pronounced her name without the final "h." Her name sounded just like "root"— the Spanish way of saying it. Some students brought their notebooks or work from the previous school year for the teacher to see.

Mr. Abeda opened the school day with the Pledge of Allegiance, which most students already knew. By noon, Jose was anxious to go home. He had repeatedly drawn two letters many times, although he had no idea what they were supposed to sound like. Ruth could print her name, and she was proud of that.

"I'll teach you letters," she told Jose.

Ruth reminded Jose of Angelica with her dark eyes, curly brown hair, and cheerful ways. That thought brought tears to his eyes. While she might be serious one minute, Ruth could break out in spontaneous laughter the next. She could laugh at herself when she made a mistake, and the other children would laugh with her.

On that first day of school, Jose spent a lot of time listening to what was going on in the other classes. The teacher would give instructions to a few students in one grade and then move on to the next. Jose, observing it all, had little time to do his assigned work.

Mr. Aveda asked one of the sixth graders, "Jimmy, will you please read the lesson aloud to the rest of the class today?" Upon hearing this, all of the children stopped what they were doing to listen.

Jimmy began talking, "A war started between the United States and Mexico. The problem that caused the war was the terrain between the Nueces and Rio Grande Rivers."

The story went on to tell about Texas when it had been an independent republic. As Jimmy finished his story, Jose thought about how well he had read. He hoped he would also be able to read well when he became a sixth grader, but that time seemed like a long way off and would involve a lot of hard work.

When he returned home that night, Jose copied the letters over and over until they turned out to be even and neat.

Paula told him, "I'm sorry that I cannot help you with those letters and sounds, Jose."

He kept reminding himself that, although he was much taller than the two other students who were in first grade, soon he would be able to write his name. That would give him the start he needed to move into other classes.

Each morning, Jose would take the five goats to eat in the field and would bring them home before he left for school. Except for weekends, he really didn't see much of Ramon.

After a few days, Jose realized that he just wasn't learning quickly enough. Remembering Vicente, the man who had given him the clothing after the flood, Jose decided to talk to him to see if he could help him with his schoolwork.

After school, Jose knocked on the door of Vicente's house. When he answered the door, Jose inquired, "Are you able to read English?"

Vicente replied, "Sure."

"Then will you teach me the sounds of all the letters?"

"Yes. When do you want to start?"

"Right away! I go to school, but I spend most of my time just copying letters. The teacher has very little time to teach first graders."

"Well," Vicente told Jose, "it gets too dark to study at night, and during early morning hours, we are all too busy. How 'bout coming to the field when I rest the oxen between twelve and two o'clock? I'll help you then."

"I must ask the teacher first, Vicente. I'm not sure if he will allow me to leave class for two hours during the day." However, Jose was anxious to get started, so he decided he would ask the teacher another time.

At his first lesson, Jose learned to write all of the vowels in the English alphabet: A, E, I, O, and U.

Vicente then said to Jose, "Now, you must practice these at home. And remember to say the sound of each vowel as you write it. After we get the vowel sounds down well, we will study the consonants and then work toward putting them together and sounding out all the letters. The next step will be to start reading the words. You will make very good progress, Jose, if you work hard."

Jose left his lesson ecstatic. Vicente had also written Jose's name in his book, and he told Jose to write it twenty times.

Rushing back to school, Jose quickly sat down in the too-small chair assigned to him. His legs even stuck out from under it. Nobody said anything, so he got started copying the letters he had learned. The three o'clock bell rang, and all the students disappeared.

Jose took off for home and arrived quickly. When he arrived, he asked Paula, "Would you like to learn to read?"

Chuckling, she said, "And who will teach me?"

"Well, I will," replied Jose.

Jose and Paula sat down, and soon they had finished the evening meal. So that the goats would eat their fill before dark, Jose took them to the fields. After they had been fed, he returned home and again studied the letters and his name, which he had written in his book.

"Now," Jose said to Paula. "I will tell you what I learned today. It's easy, really." Without waiting for a reply, he delved into the letters and their sounds. Mimicking his teacher, he said to Paula, "Now you write all of the letters in your notebook."

By the end of the first hour, she had learned all five vowels and could write Jose's name by heart. Ramon had returned home, but he paid little attention to them.

The next day at school, Jose spent more time listening to the teacher teach the other grades than he did working on his first-grade assignment. At noon, he hurried out to the fields again.

Vicente reviewed Jose on the vowels and began teaching him the consonants. In three hours, Jose had learned five consonants. Then he showed Vicente how he could write his name. Vicente seemed pleased with Jose's progress, and the farmer was also proud of himself.

The days began to get shorter, and the weather turned much cooler. It would be time for the harvest soon. Because the flood had left the ground wet and full of debris close to the river, the land there produced no crops at all. Ramon had other fields that produced a good harvest, and not having a cart of his own, he arranged for another person to bring in the corn for him.

The day of the gathering of the corn was set, and workers were hired to do the harvest. Ramon intended to pay back each man, either by working himself or lending his oxen for some fieldwork. He gave several of his big bamboo baskets to the men, who then put them on their backs. They were held in place by a tumpline around the chest and shoulders. As each man walked down a row, he would pick the corn off the stalk and toss it into the basket on his back. When it became heavy, he would empty it into the oxcart stationed strategically in the field.

It was Paula's job to feed the men once a day, outside in the field. She had done this many times and usually had someone to help her. She served the men chicken soup and fresh tortillas. After eating, they worked until the darkness overtook them.

Jose took care of the goats every day. The little ones were growing bigger and were able to eat like the three older goats. On the days when Paula had to go to the field with food for the workers, Jose stayed home from school. Nobody cared.

By Christmas, he was doing third-grade work in both reading and math. The teacher noted his keen mind and the quickness with which he understood new concepts. The lessons with Vicente continued until he harvested his own cornfield.

After the corn was harvested and piled up in the corridor, Ramon's workers went back out to the field, pulling the leaves off of each stalk and binding them into bundles. The bundles were then stored in a dry place and were fed to the animals during the long winter months. The corn on the cobs was left to dry, and little by little, it was shelled. This was difficult work. The best corn was kept for seed, and the undeveloped and odd-shaped kernels were separated and given to the animals and chickens. The dry, useless cobs were discarded, but they were never burned. The people believed you could hear the cries and pings of dead babies in the fire. It was against their tradition to burn these cobs.

The women who made tortillas bought a small quantity of loose corn daily from the stores. Jose learned that you couldn't leave corn lying around for a long time because rodents or corn weevils would destroy much of it. Rather like the planting and harvesting of grape vineyards, corn was harvested and then divided into three main categories: the white corn, which was the most preferred; next was the yellow corn; and last of all was black corn. Each type of corn had its own distinctive taste, and the farmers knew how many days each kind needed to mature.

Squash was planted between the rows of corn. Chickpeas were also planted and sometimes ground and mixed with brown cane sugar. Then a special drink could be made out of the chickpea mixture.

One day Ramon's daughter showed up unannounced. She brought Ramon a box of thin Cuban cigars, and for Paula she had brought a bolt of fine cloth for a dress. Her name was Corazon, and she was eighteen years old.

She asked Ramon and Paula, "And what news do you have to tell me?"

"Well," said Paula, "we have a young orphan boy named Jose living with us now."

Ramon then countered, "He seems quite mature for his age but is all "caught up" in school and wanting to learn all he can about reading and math. In my opinion, he needs to be paying more attention to farming and learning how to raise the animals and crops."

The next day, Corazon went to the store and purchased a spinning top for Jose. When she returned home, Corazon, Jose, and Paula sat down together.

"You know, Jose loves to carve," Paula mentioned. "In fact, he made those sticks I gave you to stir the *atole*. He seems to have a natural talent for carving."

While out on the mountainside, Jose would search for a dead copal tree. The wood was white and of just the right softness for carving. Jose enjoyed making simple carvings of animals and birds from the wood. Also, he made some stirring sticks with figures on top. About five inches long and flat like a knife, the sticks were given to Paula to stir the *atole*.

"Jose," Corazon exclaimed, "you did such a wonderful job of carving those sticks. When I return, I'll bring you some real carving tools. How would you like that?"

Jose, nodding his head, smiled broadly.

During her stay, Corazon and Paula talked incessantly about nearly everything. Paula asked many questions, such as, "What type of work do you do?" and "Are there many cars in San Antonio?" and "What types of clothes are people wearing these days?"

Next, Paula asked Corazon, "Do you have a boyfriend?"

"Yes," replied Corazon, "and I hope we will be married one day."

Paula became excited about this news, and she and Corazon continued talking for a while.

Ramon had little to say. He and Paula lived in different worlds. Ramon's world consisted of animals, land, and eating three times a day.

Paula told Corazon about Jose's coming to live with Ramon and her after his family's disappearance in the awful flood.

Paula explained, "Jose has made excellent progress in school, and I hope that he will be able to continue until he graduates from high school."

By spring, Jose could do fourth-grade work, and Mr. Aveda moved him to the proper desk. Christmas and Easter had passed, and the students began looking forward to summer vacation. One Saturday, while Jose was working in the fields, he had time to reflect on the school year.

During the Christmas season, his teacher had told the Christmas story, and the class had sung carols during the week before vacation. At home, Paula had placed a manger scene in a corner of the room. The scene depicted shepherds out on a hillside at night with some sheep lying on the ground.

Paula said to Jose, "The baby Jesus was God's Son."

When the Easter season approached, Jose noticed that the scene changed. People displayed an image of the man called Jesus, and it was carried in a procession. About all that Jose remembered about this was that Jesus was crucified and buried.

Jose asked Paula many questions about this. She listened to what he said and often admitted that she just didn't know the answer to his questions.

Also, Jose pictured a special celebration, which had occurred the previous October. The students had made paper pumpkins with faces and black cats and witches. The paper items were hung around the room for a week. This celebration was called "Halloween."

At home, Paula put food and bread on an altar. After a time, the apples dried up and the bread hardened.

When Jose asked her about it, she laughed and said, "Some people believe that the spirits of the dead come back at this time and partake of the food. If they don't find any food, they become angry and punish you. *Dia de los Muertes* is the name of this special day celebrating the saints."

Jose, thinking of his mother, murmured, "My mother never celebrated this holiday."

Finally, the last day of school arrived, and the students invited their parents to school to see the things that they had made. Then the teacher handed out report cards, recommending that each student be passed on to the next grade. He singled out Jose as having done excellent work. This made Paula very proud of him.

Jose continued thinking about some of the special things that had happened to him at school. He thought of the girl who was with him in first grade. She had made fun of him, saying, "Stupid! You can't even write your name." He felt the embarrassment of that moment once again. Later in the school year, the girl told him, "I'm sorry I called you stupid." Jose had wanted to thank her, but she had turned and walked away.

Summer passed quickly as Jose continued tending the goats and working on his carvings. Then school began again, and Jose was in the fifth grade.

During the following summer, Jose learned that they would be having a woman teacher at school. Arriving only two days before school started, the teacher stayed with the mayor and his family. She was young and not much taller than Jose, though she seemed serious and dedicated to her job. One of the things that she told the class was that she loved to ride horses. Her name was Miss Ford, and she was quite pretty. Her blonde hair appeared to have a tinge of auburn when the sunlight shone on it.

During the fall when the corn harvest began, Ramon needed Jose to help in the fields. Miss Ford didn't like it when students missed classes, and she would give them extra work to catch up with what they had missed.

At Christmas, Miss Ford did not emphasize the holiday. When school was out, she left town.

Jose grew more and more curious about Christmas and said to Paula one night, "Tell me more about this holiday."

The two sat down in the room where visitors were entertained. The big room was dark, and a single candle gave a feeble light as it burned slowly on the table. Shadows danced around them, causing a ghostly feeling everywhere.

Paula began, "From what I know about Christmas, we celebrate it because of the birth of one small child and his monumental teachings to us. Some people believe that many years ago, when Rome governed the world, a small nation called Israel was oppressed by the Romans. One cold night some shepherds stood in a field guarding their sheep. All of a sudden an angel appeared before them, telling them not to be afraid of her."

"What is an angel?" inquired Jose. "My little sister's name sounds almost like that."

"Angels don't appear very often. They live in heaven with God, and once in a while, He will send one down to earth with a special message. The shepherds were told by the angel that a baby had been born in a stable in Bethlehem. The shepherds then went to find the baby whose name was Jesus—a name that had been given to him before his birth. They found him in a stable along with his mother, Mary, and his father, Joseph."

Jose remained puzzled. "What else can you tell me, and is this story true?"

"It must be true since it has been passed down to us for thousands of years. Besides, the priest says that there's a book called the Bible that tells even more about Jesus. He grew up to become a very famous teacher and leader of some of the people. Performing miracles, he could heal the sick and bring dead people to life again. But he had enemies who were angry and jealous. These enemies convinced the Romans that Jesus was evil and should be crucified. So Jesus was betrayed by one of his own followers, whose name was Judas.

"Then some soldiers grabbed Jesus and began beating him with whips. The soldiers made Jesus carry a heavy wooden cross to a place called Golgatha. After seven horrendous hours, Jesus died. None of his friends came to his rescue or lifted a finger to help him. A man called Joseph buried him in a big tomb that was a hollowed-out rock. Three days later Jesus arose into heaven, surprising everyone."

"And then what happened?" inquired Jose.

"My goodness, you have a lot of questions! I can't read as well as you can. See if you can find that book they call the Bible, and you can read about it for yourself."

Jose's curiosity led him to wonder where he could find a Bible. He was told by some of his friends to ask the priest, but the priest came to the village infrequently. So Jose would have to wait until he could find out more about this.

One day Miss Ford told the class that they would be going on a nature hike. On the next Saturday, all the children arrived at school, eager to do something different. Miss Ford had her hair pulled back in a ponytail with a straw hat over it. She looked much too young to be a teacher.

The class hiked toward the hills. Carrying his old machete, Jose exclaimed, "Everybody watch out for snakes!" When Miss Ford heard the word *snakes*, her face paled.

The walking became more difficult due to the many tumble-weeds and bushes, but the kids kept going. After about an hour, they saw a nice, beautiful spot and decided to rest a while.

Many different birds and wild animals lived here. They spotted lizards and roadrunners. Deer, bobcat, and cougar tracks abounded here, and Jose and Miss Ford identified them for the class.

After eating their lunches, the class chatted and played together. Upon hearing a roar of thunder in the background, Jose said to everyone, "We had better be going now." No one wanted to leave, but as the thunder grew louder, Jose thought of the time when he had spent the night under the big rock.

"I can smell the rain," he said. "We'll all get wet if we don't leave now."

As they started off, thunder, lightning, and huge raindrops splattered on the bare rocks all around them. In the distance, Jose saw the outcropping of slabs of stones where he had spent a night alone.

"Let's go up there," he said loudly over the noise of the gusty winds. "We'll be safe and stay dry."

As they hurried up the hill, one of the girls cried out, "I've got a thorn in my foot!" After stopping, she was unable to walk any farther.

In a somber voice, Jose cried out, "We're going to have to carry her up the hill."

Two boys locked hands with each other, and the girl put her arms on their shoulders to steady herself. When they arrived at Jose's rock, Miss Ford looked for the thorn. All of a sudden, the sky began dumping torrents of rain on the land. Everyone watched as sheets of blowing rain swept in front of them. It became clear to all that they better stay right where they were until the storm was over. Since it was a seasonal storm, it would likely stop as quickly as it had begun.

The girl with the thorn looked concerned. "My mother will be very worried about me."

Jose asked her, "How does your foot feel?"

"Awful! The thorn is still there, and I can't walk on it," she muttered. "It really hurts!"

Jose took his knife, cut a bit of her skin, and carefully exposed the area where the thorn was located.

Someone drew a deep breath and said, "Dr. Jose Chavez."

As Miss Ford held the girl's hand, Jose worked to remove the thorn as gently as he could. It was quite large and ugly, and a small amount of blood oozed out with it. Everyone cheered, the girl's foot was bound with a clean cloth, and then she put her sandal on and stood up. She could walk again, and everybody was amazed at what Jose had done.

After a few minutes' walk, they arrived at the cave-like structure. In about thirty minutes the rain and lightning stopped, and everyone became eager to leave.

"How did you know about this spot?" Miss Ford inquired of Jose.

"I spent a night here once."

"Tell us about it."

Jose looked at her sorrowfully: "It's a long story. We had better head home. It will take us an hour to get there."

His decision was final, and the party began their way toward the village. The girl who had the thorn removed limped a little. She did not forget to thank Jose before they all dispersed.

A BUDDING ARTIST

It was 1917 and the beginning of a New Year. Miss Ford gave the class a brief history of President Woodrow Wilson's life. She explained how the United States government works between the three branches: the executive, the legislative, and the judicial. Then she explained the election and how competing individuals from the Democratic and Republican parties campaign for the purpose of winning it. Woodrow Wilson had won his presidency as a member of the Democratic Party.

Jose developed a crush on Miss Ford. He began to see her as a special person in his life, and he wanted to spend out-of-school time with her. No one called her by her first name, Elena, but Jose thought of her as a friend and wanted to call her Elena. However, she had always taught her class to be respectful of older people and teachers, so he didn't dare call her Elena. He did begin to work on a carving, though, and it was especially for her.

One day Jose was out in the fields tending the goats and saw someone walking alone. Recognizing Miss Ford, his heart began to pound inside of him as she came closer.

"I hoped I would find you here," she said. "I have been wanting to hear that long story you keep to yourself." Motioning to the nearby cave, she asked Jose, "Do you think we might go up there and talk?"

"Of course," he replied, so he put his carving away, tied the goats to a sturdy bush, and the two of them walked to the shelter of the rocks. Elena wanted to find out about the first time he had spent here. She had learned that Jose was an orphan and became curious about him.

"So you spent a night in this place?" she inquired. "What happened?"

Jose, wanting to please her, replied, "I don't find it easy to talk about."

"Maybe I can help if you will talk to me about it."

Hearing real empathy in her words, Jose drew a deep breath and wondered where all this was going.

"Take your time," she said.

For a moment, he looked thoughtful. "I was ten years old that year. My mother, little sister, and I lived close to the river just south of town. It had been raining a lot, so the river was high. One day I took the goats to the fields to let them graze. A big storm started and the goats pulled me up here. The rain stopped during the night, but I stayed here. In the morning, I went back to town and found that my house was gone. A huge wall of muddy water had washed it away." Jose stopped talking as a big lump welled up in his throat.

Elena waited silently, and then she said what he had tried to forget and could not. "Your mother and little sister died in the storm."

A big tear rolled down Jose's cheek, and he wiped it away.

"You never saw them again. How awful!"

With a shaky voice, he added, "Their bodies were never found."

Closing his eyes, he put his head in his hands. Jose and Miss Ford were silent for a while. They soon left the cave, though, and she thanked him, saying, "I'll always remember this place."

Then she left to return to town. Jose thought about their conversation some more, but he just didn't know how to handle his feelings. He knew he cared for her very much, but this was all a new experience to him.

During the following weeks, Miss Ford paid no more attention to Jose than she did to the other students, but in her heart she felt he had a special place in her life. They now shared a deep emotional bond.

The last day of school arrived, and Jose took the carving that he had finished for Miss Ford. He wanted to give it to her as a keepsake for helping him, and he decided not to present it in front of the class. He waited until everyone had gone home. When he and Elena had the classroom to themselves, he said to her, "I have made a little carving for you to thank you for being my teacher this year."

He took the wooden carving out of his shoulder bag. It was a horse's head that had been worked with great detail.

Gasping when she saw it, she finally found her voice again. "It's beautiful, and I will always treasure it. Thank you, Jose."

He dared not stay longer but left with a light heart. Feeling like he had found a true friend, he wanted to be with her more than anything else in the world.

During the summer Paula encouraged Jose to go to school in Big Town, but they had no family there with whom he could stay. Because it was too far away for Jose to walk every day, Paula decided to talk to the principal of the school and see if some arrangement could be made.

They would make another trip to Big Town. She had saved a basket of brown country eggs and also had two roosters to go to market.

After they arrived there, she inquired about the school and the man in charge of it. She was directed to an address near the school, and there she met the principal, Mr. Dickens.

"Sir," she began, "we live in Quemada, but I would like for Jose to go to school here. However, it is too far for him to walk each day. He is an excellent student. Can you help us in some way?"

Mr. Dickens remarked, "There is a boarding home close to us here where other students stay during the week. I would be glad to have Jose go to school here, and you can make arrangements with the people who run the boarding home for him to stay there. I do need to have his report cards for the past semester, though."

A man and his wife were in charge of the boarding home. They showed Paula around, and she found that the room for the boys was large and had several beds located around the four walls. Every boy had a shelf above his bed where he kept his personal items.

"The boys are expected to go home each weekend and return to school on Monday," explained the man. "The cost for room and board is two dollars a week."

Paula paid the first week's charges. She had no idea how she would pay for any other charges from the school, but she would try.

When they returned home, Paula told Ramon what had been arranged for Jose's schooling, and Ramon was opposed to the whole plan.

"School is not important," he remarked, "and every boy can make a good living on a farm. And besides, who will tend to the goats? Just when Jose is getting big enough to help me, you are sending him away from here to attend school at Big Town. I don't like it one bit."

"Ramon," said Paula, "We can sell the goats, and I will pay for his room and board."

One day, Jose announced to Paula: "I'm going to pay for some of my expenses by making carvings and selling them."

Jose spent the next few days looking at books and magazines to see how the animals should look.

When he had the time, he would work on a bird or animal carving. By the time school began, he had a large array of his creations.

"Save them until Christmas and you can sell them for more money," Paula advised him.

Ramon sold Jose's two goats that were now big and fat. Jose missed them, but he still took care of Ramon's goats until he had to leave for school. Paula and Jose made another trip to town to buy clothes and other things Jose needed.

In the boarding house there were boys in the seventh and eighth grades, as well as those in the upper classes. They all talked about how their summer was spent and what they planned for the New Year. There was a spirit of camaraderie there that Jose had not felt before with other friends. They joked and laughed among themselves and had a great time.

This school was different from Jose's old one in that there was a class for each grade and a teacher for each of the classes. Also, only English was spoken in class. Teachers would frequently assign homework to be done after school, so Jose didn't have time for much carving.

One day he could not find the knife that he had placed on his shelf with his clothes. The clothes had completely covered the knife, and he searched all around his bed, but it could not be found. He told the man who was responsible for running the boarding house. Mr. Dickens soon learned of the matter and called Jose into his office.

Looking stern and unfriendly, he said to Jose, "You are not allowed to have a knife at school or in the boarding house. Why do you need a knife?"

Surprised by Mr. Dickens's flat, haughty tone, Jose hesitated, but then he replied, "I did not know about this rule, sir. I use the knife to carve things that I plan to sell to pay part of my way through school."

Looking skeptical, Mr. Dickens was surprised to see Jose reach into his shoulder bag and pull out a carving to show the principal. "I need that knife, and I hope you will help me find it."

"I can't help you. Please don't accuse anyone and cause trouble."

Soon the whole school knew that Jose had lost his knife, but no one would help him find it. Thus, he learned an important lesson about how to take care of his personal belongings.

On Friday afternoon he started home, still dejected about the loss of his knife. After he told Paula all the details about his loss, she came up with a new idea.

"Why don't you try drawing or painting? You could make several drawings in the time it takes to do one carving."

This idea didn't appeal to Jose at first, but he took some paper and sketched a picture of a mockingbird. He did another of an ox and showed them to Paula.

"Why, you can draw too! They look very real. In time, you can use colors, and then they'll be even better."

The weight lifted from his heart and the day became clear and bright. "Thank you, Paula. I will start working even harder in my art class at school. I would also love to take music, but I believe I'll just stick to art for now."

In class, Jose became known for his budding artistry. His teacher showed him how to sketch landscapes and human faces. Part of his year became devoted to painting with watercolors and oils. The teacher gave the class pointers on how to mix colors and the proper use of brushes. Jose also continued to make sketches of the birds and animals that he knew so well. He was asked to sketch a cougar, and he looked in a book about nature to find a picture of the animal.

By Christmas, he had a group of sketches to sell. The teacher framed the cougar and put it in the classroom.

One day Mr. Dickens called for Jose to come to his office again. Opening a drawer, he pulled out a knife to show Jose.

"Somebody found this in your stuff," he said as though the incident of the knife was now closed.

"It's not mine," Jose said immediately. "Somebody planted it in my things so I would get into trouble."

"And who might that be?" Mr. Dickens asked. "Have you made enemies here?"

"Not that I know of," Jose responded. "There is one boy who resents both my artwork and my grades, but I can't say that he stole from me. I really do not suspect him."

Mr. Dickens then put the knife back in the drawer and slammed it shut. "Be gone now, Jose, and keep out of trouble. Some students just don't know how to treat others."

Upon his return to the classroom, all the students wanted to know why he had been called into the principal's office. Jose said nothing. That evening in the boarding house three boys confronted him, insisting that he tell them why he had to go to Mr. Dickens's office. Again, he didn't reply. That angered the three, and one of the boys grabbed his shirt, pulling Jose closer.

"Aren't you going to tell us?" he threatened.

Slumping to the floor, Jose could feel his heart pounding as the adrenaline surged through his body. He got up, and the boy again grabbed his collar. A button popped off.

The boy squeezed the shirt collar tightly and angrily commanded, "Speak, or else—"

With lightning speed and turning slightly to the right, Jose punched the boy in the nose. Immediately, copious tears came to the boy's eyes, and he could not see clearly. His nose began to bleed. The others heard the commotion in the room, and they saw what had happened. They all laughed aloud and one boy said, "Well, that troublemaker had it coming. Maybe he will learn his lesson now."

An upper classman then entered the room, demanding to know what had happened. The boys were not hesitant in telling him all of the details.

Turning to Jose, the boy said, "Good going. You did the right thing. If that guy should give you any more trouble, just let me know and I'll take care of him for you."

The matter was over, and everyone went back to their home-work. Jose began to feel remorseful about having hit the boy so hard. He wanted to go see how he was doing but did not.

Jose had already learned a lot this school year. He kept sketch-ing his pictures, but he longed for a knife to be able to carve again. He decided that maybe he could buy another knife and leave it at home during the week. He also wondered whether or not Corazon would come through with her promise to give him some real carving tools. He had seen pictures of them in a book used in art class.

At the end of school that year, Jose brought home his report card. When Paula saw Jose's grades, she exclaimed delightedly, "Jose, you have made me so proud of you." Cheering and dancing around the house, she was beside herself with happiness.

During this summer, Jose helped Paula with many things at home, and he also worked in the fields alongside Ramon. Jose learned to yoke the oxen together and to plow a straight furrow.

In eighth grade, he took literature and Latin. Poetry was read to the class. In addition to assigned readings, Jose read a lot more outside of class. He enjoyed reading the works of contemporary authors most of all. He also read the works of Hawthorne, Poe, Dickens, and many others. Each book or poem he read provided him a new view of the world outside his boundaries. Thus, he learned a lot. He could travel, visit other cultures, and learn about other people just by reading.

Intelligent, gifted, and precocious, Jose loved every minute of school. He was also such a friendly, outgoing person that he made many lasting friendships.

Ramon bought a horse and buggy to go to market because he found it hard to ride a donkey to town, and Paula had things to carry that were too heavy for her. A buggy was just the answer.

Big Town was growing fast because of the many people who were migrating to Texas.

Ramon, Paula, and Jose began making more frequent trips to town. The horse was gentle, and Jose wondered if it had ever been ridden or if it was used to a saddle. Ramon had failed to ask about those things when he purchased the horse.

One Saturday, Jose inquired of Ramon, "May I ride this horse?"

"Go ahead, but don't break a leg or your neck."

Jose loved horses and made friends with them quickly. His theory was that a horse that gave trouble was one that feared something. A horse could also tell if a person had a fear of them. Jose often took the horse to the fields to eat grass. He would talk to it, pet it, and treat it as if it were a person.

Jose found that he needed to stand on a rock to mount the horse. This was much easier for Jose than mounting it from the ground. Holding the reins of the bridle in one hand, he would grab the horse's mane and then jump onto it. This felt like something that he had done all his life.

His love for the horse grew ever more intense, and he knew that some students who lived only one or two miles from school rode their horses to school every day. The thought raced through his mind, *Why couldn't I ride this horse to school?*

When Jose approached Ramon with this idea, Ramon countered, "No. You just can't ride the horse to school because it is too far away. Besides, I need the horse to pull the buggy."

Jose decided that he would have his own horse someday. Plans were now in place for him to attend high school. He spent much more time combing his hair and making sure his clothes were clean and tidy. He wanted to see Elena, but their paths never crossed.

BURL AND PANCHO

During his freshman and sophomore years, Jose spent time thinking about what he should do in life. He knew he wanted to work with horses, perhaps on a ranch or where horses were trained. Besides riding Ramon's horse every chance he got, he also read a few books about the various breeds of horses and the differences between them.

One day Jose saw Elena riding the mayor's horse, and he remembered that riding horses was one of her hobbies.

As he approached her, Elena said, "Hi, Jose. I am so glad to see you again. How is school going? Why don't I take you to the mayor's house right now and he will lend you a horse so we can ride together a while?"

The two rode out to the open country, with the horses cantering and trotting where the road was level or downhill. The mockingbirds sung brilliantly, challenging each other for the most varied songs.

"I'm thinking about quitting school," Jose said suddenly to Elena.

"But why?" she asked, turning her head to see his face better. "Finish school. There is so much to know, and life goes by very quickly. I wouldn't be here teaching if I had quit."

Jose thought about what she had said, weighing his own desires against the logic of her words. "Lots of kids drop out and go to work. I have no family, and Paula has been so good to me.

It hasn't been easy for her to keep me in school, and I feel I ought to get out on my own in order to pay my way in this world."

For the first time, Elena realized that Jose was a young man, mature for his age and handsome. "What would you do? If you leave here, we may never see each other again."

The thought of this startled him. Another loss in his young life would deepen the canyon of pain in his heart. He ventured a question he had thought of many times. "Would it make any difference to you?"

She delayed her answer, not sure how to phrase what she knew to be true.

"I care for you a lot," she said softly as she stopped her horse. "You are a very good friend of mine. So I would miss you terribly, not knowing where you are or if you are okay."

Jose stopped his horse beside hers. He looked into her eyes, and she quickly looked away. Reaching for her free hand, Jose noticed that the palm was moist.

"Let me tell you something," he began somewhat shakily. "I'm a person who says what I feel, and I'm not as good at expressing my emotions or even understanding them, but I love you. I think about you all the time, and I want to be with you. I want to care for you, protect you, and always do what's best for you."

She didn't trust herself to speak but instead urged her mount to move forward. Riding on, both were lost in thought until she broke the silence.

"I'll race you to the village," she challenged.

They both broke into a fast gallop, but Jose had no desire to win the race. Arriving first, Elena slipped off her horse at the mayor's house.

"Let's talk again sometime," she said as she left.

Jose did not reply, dismounted, and began walking home.

Life became more complicated for Jose. There were so many unanswered questions in his mind, and he had no one who could help him. Continually, he thought about whether or not he should finish school. However, one night an alternative came to him.

He told Paula, "I would like to leave school for a year and work. Then I will decide if I should go back to school."

When she heard this, tears filled her eyes. "Jose," she said, "I don't understand this. What is it that makes you want to leave school?"

He replied, "I would just like to leave Quemada and find work on a ranch somewhere."

Ramon voiced his opinion. "Just when you are getting old enough to work like a man, you are going to leave us. Where is your appreciation?"

"I do appreciate everything that you and Paula have done for me, Ramon, but I think it is time for me to be out on my own, at least for a while."

Paula spoke up. "Jose has more than paid for his keep. It has been good for us to have him, and he has my blessing. Although I hate to see him leave, he is old enough to decide how to live his life. Maybe now is the time."

Jose decided when his departure date would be, and it was on a Sunday when they would take the buggy to Big Town together.

"I promise to come back to see you someday, and I will write you too."

On the day Jose left, Paula made a big lunch for him, and he placed it in his bag, along with some extra clothes. When they parted, Jose hugged Paula and both had tears in their eyes.

"I will miss you, Paula. Thanks for all you have done to help me." To Ramon, he simply waved good-bye.

Then Jose started his long walk north. As far as the eye could see, there were no ranches or farms. He felt alone and afraid. It took all of his courage to face the future.

This road was not well traveled, and he had no information about where it led. Plodding on, he wished he had a horse to keep him company and to carry his load. He thought about Elena and regretted that he hadn't done more to see her again.

A beautiful sunset suddenly appeared before him. The skies, in shades of blue, pink, and purple, sheltered the hills and valleys that were in abundance on both sides of the road. He saw no trail or path that indicated that anyone had been here recently.

While looking for a shelter where he could sleep on level ground, he suddenly felt hungry. It gnawed at him, so he ate a tortilla, wishing he had some water to drink. Lying down right where he was, he slept fitfully, waking up the next morning refreshed and ready to continue his journey.

Thirst overtook him, but he resumed walking and saw a lake shimmering on the horizon. He knew, though, that it was just a mirage. Then he came to a hill beyond which he could not see. Upon reaching the top, he saw a pond of water to one side of the road. Wagon tracks led to the pond, and Jose saw birds walking in the water along the shore. They were pecking at anything they could eat. Wondering if this was clean water, he found a sandy spot of ground near the water's edge and scooped out a hole. Water filtered into the hole, and it looked clear. He then made a second hole farther away, and the water filtered in more slowly.

Sipping a mouthful, Jose thought it tasted like rainwater. He drank more and waited. He ate another tortilla, and then he drank again. He regretted that he had nothing in which to carry the water. Jose was tempted to return to Big Town.

While looking farther down the road, he saw three men on horseback, and they were headed his way. He estimated that it would take them about forty minutes to reach the spot where he stood.

No longer feeling alone, he began walking again. Occasionally, he could see the riders when the trees along the road did not block his view. Finally, the men arrived, and Jose was glad he could talk to somebody. In his anticipation, he failed to examine the men carefully or even notice what they carried. Each had a rifle at his side and a wide belt with a pistol strapped securely around his waist. The leader rode a beautiful horse, its saddle inlaid with silver. They all showed signs of having had a hard ride, and they were all sweating profusely. Jose then stopped, moving to one side of the road.

"Where are you going?" asked the leader. Eyeing Jose up and down, he continued. "Are you running away from home?"

Hearing friendliness in the man's voice, Jose replied, "No, I'm not running away. I'm just going to look for work."

The rider was a small man, and his horse could easily carry two people, so he invited Jose to ride behind him. After some hours of riding on an up and down trail, Jose saw a path that led into the hills. The party followed it until they arrived at an old set of buildings, well hidden among the trees.

Everyone dismounted and put the horses in a corral, after which they entered a bunkhouse and enjoyed a hot meal. It consisted of meat stew on homemade bread. Eating heartily but saying very little, the men emptied their plates three or four times. Jose noticed the cook and observed that his features were strong. He was a pleasant man with a broad black mustache, and he broke into a big smile when he saw Jose.

"Welcome to the only hot meal within a hundred miles! My name is Pancho. What's yours?"

Finding his voice a bit weak from the quick turn of events, Jose answered, "I'm Jose, and your food is very good."

Jose began to wonder what these men did here in this remote, isolated place. There were no fields or signs of cattle.

After a while the men, exhausted, retired to their bunks. Pancho showed Jose where he could sleep. The bed was made of boards, and a blanket and a pillow lay at one end.

Having had a deep and restful sleep, Jose awakened quickly the next morning as the deep darkness of the night gave way to the grayish light of dawn. He got up and noticed that Pancho was moving about as he stirred up the fire and prepared the coffee.

After walking to the corral, Jose saw ten horses. The corral was an old building, and it was weather-beaten gray, having been built by homesteaders long ago. He also noticed a shop where broken bridles, saddles, and other objects hung on the wall. There was a furnace nearby, and some old, worn-out horseshoes lay on the floor.

A door slammed in the bunkhouse, and Jose saw the man who had brought him here walking toward him.

"My name is Burl," he said in a friendly tone. "I see you are up already. Did you sleep well?"

"Yes, I did," replied Jose.

Burl showed him some more of the buildings and pointed out to him the abundance of green grass that was there for the horses. A fenced-off field contained grass that was tall and ready for cutting. The hay would then be stored in the barn.

"There is always something to do around here," Burl said. "If you want some work, you can stay here. I need somebody to look after the horses when I'm gone."

They talked a while longer, and Burl found out that Jose was an orphan, that he liked horses, and that he would love to work with them.

They heard a bell ring, and Burl said, "Well, that's our breakfast call."

All the men and Jose and Pancho sat down to a well-prepared, delicious meal of tortillas and eggs. After breakfast, the men retired for the day. They worked only while they were away from the ranch.

Jose went down to the corral to become better acquainted with the horses. There, he spotted a brush and currycomb for grooming them. He began brushing one of them and did not sense any fear on the part of the horse. Talking soothingly as he touched the hindquarters of the horse, Jose removed the burrs from the mane and tail. He groomed two horses that morning and was careful to check to see if either had thorns in their hooves or any open sores anywhere.

Two days later, Burl announced, "We will be getting on the trail again today and will be taking an extra horse with us."

They never told Pancho where they were going or when they would return. This was considered secret information, although Pancho had an idea about what they did on their escapades. He had ascertained that they were bandits, robbers, and cattle rustlers.

After they left, Pancho asked Jose, "What was your life like before you met Burl?"

"It hasn't exactly been fun," replied Jose. "My family was swept away in a huge flood, and I was reared by a couple who took me in."

Pancho commented, "I had to serve jail time in San Antonio because I had no money for food or clothing. I robbed a store and was caught." Pancho wanted Jose's confidence and gained it by being honest about all that had happened to him. Then he told Jose how he could convince Burl that he really enjoyed being here at the ranch. "You need to be sure and do this because Burl is so suspicious of everyone, especially his help."

After a few days, Pancho told Jose, "You really ought to leave here. Burl will try to mold you into a man such as he is. He never had children of his own, and he wants to have a legacy, however bad. He is quite evil, however, and you don't want to be influenced by him at all. Pretend that you like it very well here and tell him you plan to stay. I'll help you get away. Listen! I'm as serious as I can be about this. If you ever have a plan about how to get away, let me know and I'll help you do it."

Jose was surprised, and he had many questions to ask Pancho. "What kind of men are they, and what do they do? Why are you here cooking for them?"

"I'll answer the last question first. During the time I was in jail, I met one of Burl's men who had been caught by the sheriff and jailed. One day Burl entered the prison when the guards and warden were busy with some rioting prisoners. I think it was pre-arranged. Anyway, Burl and his men came in with guns, ready to shoot, and they subdued the two guards, leaving them locked in a room. After they found their friend, they saw me nearby in my prison clothes.

"'Would you like to get out of here, young man?' was their question to me.

"'Of course,' I said. "I left with them and saw that they had horses ready to mount. Soon we were across the border and into Mexico. I felt fine then, but now I think I should have finished my jail sentence. I was foolish and ended up here as a captive. Burl frequently reminds me that he can turn me in at any time. But I'm going to leave one day. I'm just waiting for the right time."

Jose asked, "Why don't we leave today? They're gone."

"We need horses and supplies for the hard trip out. We may have to travel all night through trees and sandstorms and Burl will surely try to follow us. He won't mind killing us either. If we escape, he knows I might betray him by telling the authorities about him. He is a desperate man and covers all his tracks."

"How about the others? What do they do?"

Pancho laughed. "They call one of the men 'Leg.' Maybe it's because one of his legs is smaller and shorter than the other one. The other man is called 'Three Fingers.' You see, he has only three fingers on one hand. The men are Burl's stooges, doing whatever he asks them to do. They are nothing without Burl, but they are just as dangerous as he is. Don't make any of them angry. We'll lay low until Burl trusts you, and then we'll escape."

Three days went by with no sign of Burl and his men. Burl would sometimes send one of them ahead to see if everything was all right at the ranch. At other times, Burl would post a man at the exit road so no one could leave or enter. Pancho thought he knew all the angles, but he couldn't tell when the men might show up.

When Burl returned, he inspected the work done in the shop and noticed that some of the horses had begun to look better. Their manes were clean, and their hides began to shine, free of dirt and hay.

He called Jose to the corral. "Boy, you are doing a mighty fine job here, and I am proud of you. I'm very happy with the way you take care of my horses. Which one of them would you like to have for yourself? Take your pick. You may ride it whenever you like, and it will be yours."

Jose thought for a moment. "I like that mare over there in the corner."

"And why is that?" Burl inquired.

"It has personality and would never let me down. I'll bet it can climb up rocks better than any of the others."

"Take it and you can have an old saddle in the shop if you like."

Jose thanked him and went to hug his horse.

When Pancho heard all about this, he told Jose, "You see what he's doing? He wants to keep you here forever. He'll use you and then discard you like a rag."

Jose and Pancho put up some of the hay before it got too dry. Hard work was required to cut the hay with a scythe and then move it into the barn. While they worked, they talked—sometimes in English and sometimes in Spanish.

"Where did you learn to cook, Pancho?"

"I became one of the cooks at the jail when some of the men who had been cooks were released. I also became an expert at baking bread, and it was a big hit with all the men."

"Well, tell me about how you came to have no food or clothing and robbed the store."

"Because I got mixed up with the wrong gang," replied Pancho. "I had a good family, and they sent me to school and gave me everything I needed. But I started running around with the wrong types of boys and I left home. We had to steal clothing and food to eat. My parents were shocked and almost disowned me. They never came to visit me. I'm sure they must have read about my escape in the paper. They probably thought I had become a real criminal, involved with the worst of men. But I learned a lot in prison. I studied all I could and read every book in the library." Pancho paused and then he added sadly, "I never saw my family again."

Jose heard the sadness in Pancho's words and felt the pain he was experiencing.

"What book did you like the most, Pancho?"

"I liked the New Testament best. It will change your life for the better if you will follow what it tells you to do. I didn't want to read the book just for myself. When I finished it, I wanted to tell other people about Jesus Christ and how He came to save the world. I still have the New Testament that I received in jail."

Jose was curious about this New Testament. "Show it to me. I have heard a little about Jesus, but I have never read anything about Him."

Pancho spoke very seriously, "Don't let Burl or his men catch you reading that book. They hate it because it tells people all about right and wrong. No one likes to hear what they are doing wrong, so watch yourself."

That night Pancho gave Jose the little book, and he began to read. At about the same time, Burl and his men returned and brought Pancho the supplies he needed. All of them, including the horses, looked worn out and in need of a good rest. There was tension in the air whenever they were present at the camp. They were obviously under stress, and any little thing could provoke a real crisis. Jose went about his business every day, and Burl noticed his work, continuing to be pleased with him.

During one of the times when Burl and Jose were talking, Burl told him, "If you need anything like clothes or boots, let me know, and when I am in town, I'll get them for you."

Jose had never talked to Burl about what he would get for working. His needs were not many, though he would like to have a pocketknife. When Burl found out about this, he brought Jose a good three-bladed knife. It was sharp, would do a good job in fixing leather objects, and it could also be used for carving.

When Pancho heard about this, he told Jose, "He's trying to buy your loyalty. He wants to make you feel as if you owe him something so you won't want to leave here."

Pancho smiled, yet his voice was totally sincere. He was thinking about the details of their escape: the supplies they would need and possible obstacles that they would encounter. He made some beef jerky and stored it secretly for the time when they would need it.

Jose and Pancho worked together on things that needed to be done around the ranch. The barn needed some repairs, and hay had to be put inside the barn.

Pancho still needed to get a horse and a few shells for his gun. This would serve to kill small game in case they had no food out in the wild country. To leave camp when Burl was gone would not be difficult, and he could take one of Burl's horses. No doubt, Burl had taken the horses from someone else. That didn't make it right, of course, but if Pancho's future plans worked out, Burl would not need any of the horses.

The day came when it was obvious that Burl was going on another trip. The horses had rested, and the men had repaired broken straps. After doing some target practice with the rifle and pistol, Pancho and Jose washed their clothes. Pancho prepared some tortillas and beef jerky that they could eat on their journey.

The party left early one morning, and Pancho said to Jose, "Get ready, because we are leaving here tonight. We must be on the alert at all times to be sure Burl and his men are not hiding along the trail somewhere. This is going to be a full moon night, and it seems like the perfect time to go."

Toward midnight, they set out on their horses. Not being able to take the same trail that Burl used, they proceeded through a dark forest where there were no trails.

As they came to some thick bushes, Jose remarked to Pancho, "It would be easier for you to get through these bushes if you would quit eating so much of that bread that you bake!"

Pancho said nothing. He was busy keeping the branches out of his face.

Suddenly, they both became frightened that Burl and his men might double back and find out that they were missing. In this case, Burl would surely find them, take them back to camp, and keep them in slavery forever. And—as spooky as it may seem— he might even murder them!

They didn't stop until about three hours after they had started out. Finally, they decided to rest their horses. Pancho said, "I am going to scout around and see if I can find the trail. We must be going in the right direction because we are following the North Star."

Suddenly, they saw fresh horse tracks and tried to figure out if the tracks were going north. That might indicate that Burl's men had gotten suspicious and started looking for them.

At daybreak, Jose said to Pancho, "Let's search for a place to hole up because we really need some sleep. Why not head into the hills? We also need to find water for the horses."

Meanwhile, after arriving back at camp, Burl discovered that the boys were not there. Determined to find them, he could not believe that they would dare leave the ranch. Obviously he had misjudged their intentions. Becoming angry at himself for having been taken, he called his men together.

Racing from the hideout, the group intended to overtake Pancho and Jose. They had to go up and down hills and travel through rocky spots and wet sand. They also continued to look for fresh horse tracks.

After searching for what seemed like hours, Burl and his men decided that they had been outwitted and returned to the ranch.

ALBERT AND LUCILLE

Jose and Pancho were still worried about Burl and his men finding them. The trees hid the horses fairly well, and there was plenty of grass for them to eat. They ate some of the food they carried and drank from a nearby stream. After watering the horses, they traveled until daylight again until they found a safe place to spend the day. A wall of sand and rock surrounded this place on three sides, and on the fourth side, a small stream of water flowed down into the valley. Then it flowed into a forest of mesquite trees so anyone looking for water would be drawn to this larger stream.

After they had unsaddled the horses and dropped the reins, Pancho said to Jose, "You go to sleep and I'll watch for a while. Then I'll wake you up to watch while I sleep."

Before Jose slept, he thought about Elena and wished she were here to enjoy the view with him.

When he awakened in late afternoon, Pancho was still sitting on a high point of the wall.

"You never woke me up," Jose chided him. "Did you think I would fall asleep if I watched?"

Pancho didn't answer but stood up and looked searchingly in the direction of the road. "I sure hope we don't see Burl and his men. Our supplies are getting low too, and we are going to have to find some more."

"Well, Pancho, we're certainly not close to anything around here. It's all open country, and we haven't even seen any lizards or rattlesnakes to eat."

As he began looking farther down the road, Pancho noticed some signs of a small town or a bunch of ranch buildings in the distance. They appeared to be directly ahead. "I wonder if Burl is in those buildings farther down the road."

"Perhaps, but we won't know until we get there. We may as well continue our journey."

Before leaving, however, Pancho suggested that they sit down and read a passage from the New Testament. Jose began to read. "Let not your heart be troubled. You believe in God; believe also in me. I go to prepare a place for you so that where I am, there you may be also" (John 14:1, NIV).

He quickly stopped reading. "What does this mean?"

Pancho ventured an answer. "Here, Jesus is telling his followers not to be afraid when He returns to the Father. The disciples knew they soon would be orphaned, just as you were, Jose."

"Pancho, have you ever been afraid?"

"Yes, sometimes when I fail God by not doing the right thing, I am afraid of Him. However, I know for sure that I will spend eternity with God. He tells us that if we believe in Him and accept his Son, Jesus, as our personal Savior, we will be His forevermore. This is very plainly put in the Bible when Jesus says, 'I am the way and the truth and the life. No man comes to the Father except through me'" (John 14:6, NIV).

Jose commented, "God will always be with us wherever we go and whatever happens to us. Pancho, at my age, what are the important things I should be doing to honor God? You know, I like so many stories that I read about Jesus in the New Testament. I guess my favorite story is about how Jesus died but then rose from the grave. I also like the story about the woman at the well and how Jesus healed her from her sins. We are told about Jesus's disciple, Peter, who left jail with the help of an angel. Parts of the New Testament make me feel sad, as though I am guilty in God's eyes."

Looking Jose in the eye, Pancho said, "You are. Have you loved God with all your heart every day of your life? If you haven't, you have broken his laws."

"You say God loves us. It also says that in the Bible. If that is true, then why is there so much sadness in the world? Why did we have the flood that took away my mother and sister? And is Burl pursuing us because he wants to harm us?"

Pancho drew a deep breath. "You do have some hard questions. Most of the trouble in the world is due to man himself. He chooses to do wrong on many occasions. Man's jealousy, greed, hate, and pursuit of sensual pleasures all are sins. I am just like other men also. I have had some of those same problems, but I prayed to God, and my heart changed. Jesus saved me and gave me a new heart and a desire to please only Him. That doesn't mean I'm perfect, but I hope you can see that I am different. Have you come across the verse in the Bible that tells us about how, if a person is united with Christ, he is a new person? We are told that old things are passed away and the new have come."

The setting sun reminded them that it was time to be on their way. A glance at the road ahead revealed no activity to worry about.

Once on the road, they saw a small building that looked like a store. It was closed, though, so they knocked on the door. Somebody looked out through a crack in the side of the wall, and soon the door opened.

"Could I buy some food?" Pancho asked. He noticed the few shelves behind the counter. There were the usual things that are needed by rural people. In front, there were some toasted pieces of bread, cheap cookies, and dried raisins.

The man who opened the door cried out to a woman in the back, "Do we have any tortillas left to sell?"

Pancho looked out the door in a southward direction. "Have you seen three men on horses come by here?"

"They were here a couple of hours ago," the man said. "Are they your friends?"

"No," Pancho replied quickly. "They are chasing us. Where did they go? Do you know?"

"They just asked me about the road ahead and if it led to a decent-sized town."

"One of them is a famous bandit and cattle rustler," Pancho told the man. This statement seemed to lessen the suspicion that the man had shown toward them in the beginning. Pancho continued, "I will have some tortillas, beans, and sardines."

"Let's head deeper into the hills," Pancho suggested.

The next day Jose commented, "It looks as if there have been some cattle that came through here. I also see a ranch house nearby and maybe two or three other buildings."

They rode up to the main building. Pancho dismounted and, with his hands in full view, went toward the door. An old man came out carrying a gun. He pointed at Pancho, but he couldn't tell whether or not it was loaded.

He said to the man, "Can my friend and I stay here tonight? Our horses need rest, and we won't cause you any trouble."

The man looked at their horses and saw that they were not carrying any weapons. His voice was friendly, and in a pleasant manner, he said, "Go put those horses in the barn. There's hay for them in there. My name is Albert, and I'll introduce you to my wife, Lucille."

After Albert introduced the boys to Lucile, she continued to prepare the lunch that she had been making.

"Where are y'all headed?" Albert asked.

"We're thinking about Lubbock. How far away is it?" asked Pancho.

Albert thought about this for a minute. "I would say it's at least a three-day ride from here."

"Well, Albert, how big is your ranch, and how are things going?" questioned Pancho.

Jose was observing the terrain and the beauty of the land. He looked around and saw some cattle grazing in the distance. It couldn't be easy for Abert and Lucille to make the trip to the nearest town.

"I'm thinking about selling it," said Albert. "I work alone and have no one here to help me. Also, I can't ride the range like I used to, and I really should sell the cattle. I need to move them to market before the cold weather sets in."

Everybody enjoyed the delicious home-cooked meal. As afternoon wore into evening, Albert addressed Jose and Pancho. "I take it you have no job right now. How would you like to help me round up my cattle and take them to market? I can pay you after the sale since I don't have much cash."

Pancho replied for both himself and Jose. "We'll let you know in the morning." The two retired to the barn and put out their bedrolls.

"It would be a good way to get Burl out of our lives," Jose suggested.

"You know, Jose, when I was alone at the hideout after Burl and his men would leave, I prayed that God would send someone to help me escape. Then you came. God answered my prayer, just like it says in the Bible. Now He has answered me again."

The next morning, Jose got up early and went outdoors. He walked around and noticed a small grave near a tree. A small cross in the ground marked the grave, but he couldn't read the name that was on the cross. He also noticed that all the buildings around the farm were too large for a single family to be living here alone. He decided that, at one time, this had been a busy, prosperous place.

Albert came into view, and he was repairing fences. Some wires were down, and a post needed replacing here and there. The wooden gate seemed to be all right. Cattle driven from the right direction would just naturally enter the gate and be penned in an area where they could eat grass and drink water.

As they ate their breakfast the next morning, Lucille asked Pancho and Jose if they had slept well. "I can give you more blankets if you need them. We just want you to be comfortable here."

After breakfast, the three men mounted their horses as Albert led the way. In addition to the ropes they all had that were tied to each saddle, Albert had a bullwhip that sounded like the crack of a rifle. He used it to get the cattle moving, although about half a dozen seemed content to stay where they were. Covering some rough country as they continued their ride, the men avoided the deep canyons and rocky outbursts. That afternoon they located a dozen animals in a lush valley where there was plenty of water. They appeared to be in good shape and paid no attention to the men.

"We'll make camp," Albert said, "and get them started early in the morning."

They lit a fire, heated some tortillas, and Albert made some strong coffee. Jose was overjoyed to be on his first cattle drive. Their plan was to move all the cattle back to the ranch, brand the young ones, and sell the others.

Early the next morning, they started their hard work. Albert's horse was old and knew how to move cattle, but Pancho's horse had to be guided for every move. Jose's horse, on the other hand, had obviously been trained to work with cattle. It would quickly keep an animal from straying or bolting away from the others.

Using his whip, Albert got the cattle's attention and started them moving. Calling out to the cattle in a rough voice, Pancho let the critters know where he was and urged them to go. An old crooked-horn animal became the leader, and the others followed reluctantly. Sometimes an animal would turn and make an attempt to go back to the valley, but a loud crack of the whip usually got it going again.

At noon, when the group came across the cattle they had passed the day before, Albert stopped to give the cattle some rest. They began to graze while the men rested in the shade of a big tree. Finally, they headed toward the ranch again and arrived there in late afternoon.

When they took the cattle to market the next morning, they were all sold to one man who planned to ship them to Saint Louis or Chicago. Albert took the cash and stuffed it into his money belt. They returned home and began preparations for another trip to the farthest edge of the ranch.

"This will take three or four days," Albert told them.

Before they started out the next morning, a stranger arrived on horseback. The star pinned to his shirt said "Marshal."

"Where are you guys headed?" he asked.

"We're rounding up my cattle for market," replied Albert.

"Let me go with you," said the marshal. "There are reports that cattle are being stolen in these parts. Brands are being erased and changed."

Their plan was to head for high country and make a sweep south to look for cattle. When they reached the boundary of Albert's ranch, they saw a hill that was somewhere nearby. The marshal noticed a thin blue cloud of smoke rising from beyond the rim. Taking only a few minutes to reach the top of the hill, he could see that it was just as he had suspected: men were branding cattle down below.

Returning to Albert, Pancho, and Jose, the marshal said, "I plan to arrest those men. Tie your horses here in the trees and walk with me quietly to the top. I'm making you deputies—authorities of the state." He pinned a star on Pancho's shirt and another on Albert's. He said to Jose, "You stay with the horses here and bring me one when I call for it."

As he gave his rifle to Pancho, he said, "Do not fire this, but point it toward the men. You all stay at the rim of the valley with your heads peeking over the edge and align the gun so that the men can see it. I'm going down to arrest them, and I hope there won't be any shooting. Good luck and wish me well."

The marshal walked away as quietly as he could. The animal that the men were branding was bellowing and making a lot of noise. Pancho saw three men: two were hunched over the animal, and one was heating the branding iron in the fire. Their horses were tied a distance away from them, and their guns were hung on the pommels of the saddles.

The lawman drew close and, with his gun drawn, commanded in a loud voice, "Don't move and don't go for your guns."

The men looked up, startled by the harsh words spoken with authority and power. They noticed the star on the marshal's shirt and looked around to see if anyone else was there.

"The men are up here," the marshal called, nodding toward the place where two men's heads peered over the rim. The sheriff called Pancho to come down, and as he covered the men with his gun, he put handcuffs on each of them. He then locked them in place so that they could ride their horses.

Other rustlers were making noises in the distance as they brought in cattle to be branded. The marshal called to Jose to bring his horse and for Albert to come down and identify the animal they had been working on.

"That's my brand," he told the marshal.

The men glared at him and swore about their bad fortune. They knew rustlers were jailed for long terms and sometimes hanged until dead. The first man, as stubborn as the cow he had been working on, refused to mount his horse.

"You'll have to put me on," he said.

The marshal picked up the hot branding iron and approached him. "You had just better get on that horse right now or you will be in even bigger trouble than you already are." He took the rifle from Pancho. "It's time to move on now. I've got to get these men to jail."

All of this happened so quickly that Albert had no time to give way to his emotions. As the four horses disappeared, Albert, Pancho, and Jose broke out in uncontrollable laughter. The other rustlers must have guessed something was wrong and fled. Looking around the branding spot, Pancho noticed that it must have been used for a long time. The grass was worn down, and a bare spot of dirt showed several colors of cow hair on the ground. Somebody had killed a young cow and hung up strips of meat to dry. Albert helped himself to as much as he could easily carry, and they began looking for cattle. It took the rest of the day to bunch together about fifteen head of cattle, and Albert looked pleased. If he could get these critters to market, he would be more than happy.

The next morning, work started early. Albert was cracking the whip and getting the cattle together. Again, he looked for a lead animal that the younger animals could follow. With some difficulty, they got out of the valley and headed toward the ranch. It was a long, slow, tedious journey. By nightfall, the cattle were in the corral and had settled down for the night.

The three men prepared to brand the few young calves the next day. This was disagreeable work, and the hot irons seared the skin of the animals. The "burnt hair" smell was awful. Al would lasso the animal's front feet, and then he and Pancho tied all four feet together. Jose kept the branding irons hot.

By afternoon, the branding was finally finished. Each animal bore the Beta letter of the Greek alphabet on its left hip. Now they were ready to be let loose on the range. Albert decided that if he got a good price for his animals, he would buy some more fencing and keep his cattle where he could easily find them.

The second bunch of animals went to market as the first had done. Albert said to Pancho and Jose, "I'm a gonna get my money and hire a wagon and driver to take some fence wire and steel posts out to the ranch. Let's fence in several acres of land where there is good grass and water."

As Pancho got better acquainted with the ranch, he loved it. *This would be great for a horse ranch*, he thought to himself and told Jose, "If Albert ever wants to sell out and I have any money, I want to buy this land."

As for Albert, he seemed rejuvenated with the sale of his cattle and knew there were other cattle of his out on the range. He said to Pancho and Jose, "Let's go out again but to another part of the range. Every inch of this valley needs to be looked over very carefully."

They came upon some of Albert's cattle that had the brand altered. On the Greek letter Beta, somebody had carefully imposed the Greek letter Alpha. Albert had never heard of nor seen any such brand before. After rounding up about fifteen more head of cattle, the men took them back to the ranch. This time when the animals were taken to market, some of the buyers were men Albert had never seen. Two of them examined Albert's cattle and then claimed that three of the cattle belonged to somebody else—a man with the initials BZ.

"Whose brand is that?" Albert demanded.

The men said nothing but insisted that Albert give them up. He refused. The constable who was monitoring the sale heard the discussion and insisted the two men give the name for the BZ brand.

"His name is Burl Zadot," one of them said. "He seldom comes up here himself except to collect money".

Upon hearing this, a bright light went on in Pancho's head. *So Burl's business extends way up here*, he thought.

Albert talked to the constable, and everybody heard the conversation. "These are my cattle. Look at the brand and you will see that it's the letter Beta. Whoever is at fault here just put two lines over the vertical part of the letter and extended it downward. That's what makes it look like a Z."

The sale continued, and Albert got his money. Pancho examined the two men carefully in case he should ever meet up with them again. He told the constable, "The area where those animals were located is near the state line."

The constable replied, "I will inform the marshal. It is his job to investigate cattle rustling."

When Albert, Pancho, and Jose arrived home at last, Albert was not feeling well at all, and he was worse the next day. Pancho suggested, "Jose and I can go out and look for more of your cattle."

Albert said, "Go right ahead, and maybe I will feel a lot better when you get back here."

Pancho and Jose left and went in a different direction than the day before. They rounded up four or five "B" cattle and drove them into a valley to join Albert's other cattle. They spent the night out under the stars.

Sleep did not come easily to Jose that night, so he began talking to Pancho.

"Have you ever been in love? I mean with a woman."

"Why? Are you in love?"

"Well, I was in love with my teacher, Elena, when I was in school. I really cared for her a lot, but after that year, I never saw her again. What about love? Does it die if the one you love doesn't love you? I felt rejected, yet I felt that she cared a little about me."

Pancho chose his words carefully. "Do you remember that part of Corinthians where it says, 'Love is patient, love is kind. It does not envy, does not boast, it is not proud. It is not rude, it is not self-seeking. It is not easily angered, it keeps no record of wrongs. Love does not delight in evil but rejoices with the truth. It always protects, always trusts, always hopes, always perseveres. Love never fails' (1 Corinthians 13:4-8a, NIV). I believe that if you truly love somebody, you will always love them. Those words were written by the Apostle Paul, and I think they have two meanings. This love refers to not only the love that a man and a woman have for each other but also to the type of love that human beings—all of us—should have for each other."

Jose again thought of his mother and Angelica. "Why did my mother and little sister have to die in the flood?"

Pancho seemed puzzled by this question. "I don't have the answer to that question. Ask God about it. Pray and see if he gives you an answer."

"Do you think He cares?" Jose asked.

"Of course. He is interested in all that you are and do. Let me tell you something. There are three very important decisions each person has to make in life. First, we must put Jesus first in our lives. Second, we must marry the right person and the one God wants us to. And third, we must choose the proper life work for ourselves. All of these things are very important, and God will help us to make the right decisions if we will only pray and follow what He tells us to do."

Jose's head nodded, and he was soon fast asleep.

The next day, Pancho awoke early, grabbed his rifle, and went hunting. He had seen some wild turkeys the day before and wanted to shoot one.

As noiselessly as he could, he walked under some trees nearby. Seeing a turkey roosting on a limb and taking careful aim, he pulled the trigger, and the bird fell to the ground. When he got back to camp, he cleaned the bird quickly. After finding a green stick, he made a spit for roasting the turkey. After it cooked for hours, Pancho and Jose took only a few minutes to eat the whole thing, as well as some tortillas they had carried.

Afterward, the two saddled the horses and Pancho used the whip to get the cattle moving. Jose's horse did double duty that day, and they were able to get the cattle home before dark. Some were unbranded, so Albert had to verify that they were his.

Pancho and Jose made two more trips to find more of Albert's cattle while Albert recovered.

Albert proposed that they stay for a couple of days longer so that they could start out rested and with clean clothes.

Jose said to Albert, "Tell me about the grave under that nearby tree."

"That is the grave of our only child, Ester. Lucille took it very hard and still grieves about it to this day, even though it happened long ago."

Jose felt deeply for the woman who had looked forward to raising her own child. She had lived a lonely and hard life on the ranch, miles from neighbors with whom she could talk. He saw in her some of Paula, as well as his mother, Hanna.

Putting his arm around Lucille, he said, "I lost my little sister and my mother when a flood swept them away. I know how you feel about your little girl, but I'm sure she must be happy living with Jesus."

He took a small carving of an angel from his pocket and handed it to her. "Keep this as a remembrance of our stay here. Thank you for all the things you did for us."

Lucille cried. "Thank you for saying that," she whispered.

Albert paid the two of them well and wished them luck.

ANOTHER LOSS

It was hard for Pancho and Jose to leave those they had learned to love.

They rode in silence for a while until Jose said, "I want to come back here someday to visit. How about you?"

Pancho nodded and said, "You know, I really would like to buy that ranch." Jose knew—it was only the tenth time Pancho had told him.

The two looked forward to whatever lay ahead. The bond of friendship between them was strong, and Pancho worried about a time when they might have to separate.

They rode on and observed ranches as they passed them along the road. Meeting no one, they soon stopped for the night about two hundred feet from the road.

Jose said, "What are your plans when we get to Lubbock?"

"I'm going to turn myself into the first Texas Ranger I see. I'll tell him who I am and all about Burl's activities."

Jose was quiet for a while and then commented, "But you may go to prison again. We'll be separated, and who knows where you'll be?"

Pancho didn't answer, and Jose soon fell asleep. The two slept until dawn.

As they started out the next day, Jose remarked, "I wonder how far we will get tonight."

"I don't know," said Pancho, "but I'm hungry. It's about noon, so let's stop and eat."

They finished the last of the food they had carried from Albert and Lucille's. A lone horseman came by from the direction in which Pancho and Jose were headed.

"How far is it to Big Spring?" asked Pancho.

"Oh, about four hours, and there is a small town before that," replied the man.

Upon arriving in Big Spring, they found a place to stay, food to eat, and a place to feed the horses.

Pancho said, "I have got to go to the barber and get my hair cut."

Jose looked around and found a clothing store, and when Pancho returned, they both bought new clothes and boots. Pancho's face was cleanly shaven, and his mustache was neatly trimmed. Then they saw their first car, a 1916 Hudson, parked in front of city hall. As others before them had done, they both examined it closely. Cars were scarce in that part of the country; roads were bad and auto shops didn't exist.

On one of their trips about town, Pancho noticed a sign that said "Marshal's Office," but he was not quite ready to turn himself in just yet.

The two went to the post office, where Jose bought an envelope, stamp, and paper. He wanted to write to Paula and Ramon. While there, they saw mug shots on the wall that said "Men Wanted." One of them especially stood out. It was none other than Burl Zadot. Beneath the picture in big, bold letters were the words: "Two hundred dollars to anyone giving information leading to the arrest and conviction of this man."

Jose read it, whistled, and said to Pancho, "Look! We can get a reward!"

"Yeah. The law is gonna catch up with that man yet."

From there, they walked to where they saw a sign that said "Help Wanted." They saw all sorts of opportunities, but none of them involved working with horses, so Jose was not interested.

That night, Pancho spoke. "I am ready to turn myself in to the law, but not until after you find work. Here's my rifle, and if they take me away, the horse is yours. I'm sure I won't need him."

Jose wrote his letter to Paula and told her all about the experiences he and Pancho had enjoyed together. He told her about seeing the automobile and then added, "If you see Elena, tell her I'm well and I think of her often."

After mailing the letter, he and Pancho headed for the horse market. Sellers and buyers were haggling over prices. A buyer would open a horse's mouth and check its teeth.

"Why do they do that?" Jose asked Pancho.

"So they can tell the horse's age. If the back teeth are well worn down, the horse is old, and if the teeth are not all showing, the animal is fairly young. Just like a small child, they don't have all of their teeth right away. The back teeth come in last."

After asking around, they could find no one who wanted a ranch hand. As they returned to their room, Pancho was deep in thought. "If you sell my horse, you will get at least forty dollars, Jose."

"You talk like you are leaving right now," said Jose with disappointment in his voice.

"We'll see what the Texas Ranger says when he comes here. Rumor has it that he should arrive here soon. One of two things will likely happen when I confess: they could put me back in prison or they might want me to take them to where they can find Burl. I can tell them about the hideout and a lot of things that will help them find him and arrest him without any loss of life. After that, they will have to decide about my unfinished sentence."

The next day, Jose posted a piece of paper on the employment office board that read "Looking for Work with Horses." However, there were also many houses being built around town, and Jose considered that perhaps he could also qualify to work as a carpenter.

Looking disheartened, he sat down next to Pancho on a bench close to the town hall.

"Don't be discouraged," Pancho said. "It may take a little more time than we think it should."

That afternoon, a man approached the two. "I hear you are looking for work," he said, looking at Jose. "I have a ranch about ten miles west of here. I raise mainly horses, although I do have a few head of beef. Have you worked with horses?"

"I have," Jose replied modestly. "I also have my own horse."

Now eyeing Jose with skepticism, the man continued. "How old are you, son?" he asked.

"I'll soon be seventeen," he replied.

Pancho listened and then spoke up. "You will be happy with this fellow. He learns fast and is very dependable."

They continued talking for a while, and Jose learned that he would not be expected to work on Sunday. Also, he would come into town once a month with the rancher and return to the ranch the following day.

"Well, I guess you're hired, son. By the way, my name is Sommers." They shook hands on this, and Jose told Mr. Sommers that he would be ready to go back to the ranch with him the next morning.

Next, they went to the marshal's office to find out when a Ranger might be coming. "There is one here now," said the marshal, "and I'll call him for you."

Pancho and Jose were ushered into a room, and soon the ranger arrived. They saw before them a tall, thin man dressed in uniform and hat.

"What do you want of me?" asked the Ranger.

Pancho began, "My name is Francisco Cruz, and I can tell you where you will find Burl Zadot, or at least where he was a few days ago. I know nothing about his activities recently, although I worked for him and his gang as a cook for a while."

Looking surprised, the Ranger spoke quickly now. "Tell me right from the beginning all that you know about that desperado."

"Well," Pancho continued, "a long time ago I was imprisoned for robbing a store. Burl had a friend in the same prison, and one day, after some guns had been smuggled in to him, he overtook the guards, escaping with his friend. I happened to be there near the door, and he asked me if I wanted to leave also. Of course I took him up on the deal. Two horses were waiting outside when we left, and we escaped across the border. We hid out near Mexico for a time, and then we found a place near Big Town. It is south of here and well concealed in the hills. I started cooking for Burl and his men. There were usually three or four of them besides Burl. From his hideout they would rustle cattle and rob banks and stores. He is really a desperate man.

"One time Burl told me, 'Ain't no lawman never gonna arrest me! I'll die before I'll let that happen.' That is how I met Jose here. Burl hired him to take care of his dozen horses. Jose had no idea what Burl did for a living. We both waited months for the right time to leave Burl, and a few weeks ago, we left. He hunted for us, but we evaded him by living in the hills and traveling at night."

The Ranger looked at Pancho and said, "You know there is a reward out for this Burl. Is that what you want?"

"No," said Pancho emphatically. "I want to help put him behind bars. I can lead you to the place and tell you all about the hideout. It won't be easy to capture him, but it is possible."

Belief slowly crossed the Ranger's face. "Let's get out of here, you and I. We will have to act fast. Burl may have gone elsewhere by now."

Pancho and Jose embraced.

"I'll see you again soon," said Pancho. "But if I don't see you, you'll know where I am."

"Take me with you," implored Jose. "I can help."

"No way!" Pancho responded heartily.

Jose felt saddened by this turn of events. Another friend he loved was gone. He wondered, *Is this the way it is with orphans? When you make a real friend, you lose him.* He went to his room and collected his things. Guy Sommers would be ready to leave by eleven o'clock the next morning.

Jose took out the New Testament that Pancho had left for him. He became encouraged to know that God would take care of all his needs if he would seek God's kingdom first. "But seek first his kingdom and his righteousness, and all these things will be given to you as well" (Matthew 6:33, NIV).

Before he went to sleep, he prayed. "Please, God, take care of Pancho."

The next morning, Jose went to the library to see what books he could borrow. He wanted something to read during the long evening hours and on nasty days when the weather was too bad to work outdoors.

The trip to the ranch was uneventful. The road, very well traveled, was actually the old Comanche trail. About five miles before getting to their destination, Jose noticed a single building off the road. The sign out front said "Christian Church." It was a small building with a few shade trees nearby. An iron hand pump indicated that there was water there. Jose noticed other ranches off in the distance. The country was fairly flat with high hills farther away.

Mr. Sommers showed him where he could put his horse and where he would be staying. His room was a part of the main house, but it had its own access to the outside. At mealtime, Jose met Mrs. Sommers and their two children—Jack, twelve years old, and Jennifer, ten years of age. Both the Sommerses wondered how this new man, who looked so young, was going to work out. Ranching was demanding work that required long hours.

Jose asked the children about their school.

"We study at home," Jack said.

Mr. Sommers showed Jose the horse barn and pointed out the fences that divided the different types of horses. Some were for general riding; some were quarter horses that were used for racing; and some were ponies, for families. None of them were ready to be sold and would have to be trained. Sommers was known in the community as a rancher who had good horses. He and Jose talked about Pancho's horse that they had brought with them.

Jose told Mr. Sommers briefly how he had come to have it and asked him what he should do with it. Mr. Sommers agreed to keep it for a while.

The next day, a neighbor showed up saying he needed a horse because one of his had been injured. Jose showed him Pancho's horse. The man examined it carefully, rode it, and then decided to buy it.

Jose asked forty dollars for it and said, "If you don't like it after a week, bring it back and your money will be returned."

"More than fair," was the man's grateful response.

Sommers had some work to do around the house and told Jose, "Feel free to look around. You may ride or walk to the corrals. However, be careful of the wild mustang, gray in color, because he can be very dangerous. If you go near him, he will put his head down and kick up his hind legs in defiance. Better stay away from him."

Jose started by spending time with the smaller ponies, many of which had never been bridled. He knew he would have a lot of work to do. The gray mustang was beautiful. When Jose entered the pen, he talked to the horse but never faced it directly. When the mustang moved, Jose moved parallel to him and talked to him in a low, calm voice.

The saddle horses were a mixed lot. They didn't seem to mind Jose's being there. He wondered where all these horses had come from.

Mr. Sommers and Jose worked together most of the time for the first week.

One day the rancher said, "We have to get a couple of ponies ready for a family in Big Spring. They have ordered them for their kids. That means that they will have to be gentle and broken in to ride. Pick out one, lead it around, and get it used to following you."

Jose brushed the horse, talked to it, and put a saddle on its back the next day. Accepting the saddle, the horse and Jose walked around together. Jose put a twenty-pound bag of sand on its back. That wasn't much weight, but the horse got used to having a weight on his back. After he had led the horse around for an hour, it began to show signs of being tired. The same routine continued for a few days with more weight being added each day.

"Who is going to ride that pony?" Jack asked his dad at the dinner table one night.

"We'll see, son. It will be either Jose or me."

"And may I ride it when it's been broken in?" he asked.

"You can ride my horse any time," Jose told him.

His mother looked worried. She didn't want to chance her boy's getting hurt. "I don't think so," she told Jack. "And that's final!"

Jose wondered why she was so fearful. Guy was different. He took risks and didn't overly protect the kids from a little danger.

The next day, Jose saddled up the horse for riding.

"Go ahead," Guy said to Jose. "I think he's ready."

Jose talked to the horse and, with a smooth mount, was on its back. The horse was startled but didn't try to buck or throw him off. Jose urged it forward, and the two were on their way down the road. All that remained for Jose to teach him were the signals from the rider: when to stop, when to turn, and so forth. These were all important commands. He continued to train the pony while working with a second horse. Both horses had good dispositions and were dependable. When Guy sold them, they were in top condition.

During the week that followed, Jose worked with the saddle horses. Some of them had been broken in, so he gave them workouts. Other horses needed to be trained to be led and to be saddled. Once in a while, he caught a glimpse of the gray bronco and became determined to make friends with it.

One day he was riding his own horse and entered the fenced area. The mustang listened when Jose spoke to him. He urged his horse to get near the bronco, but he shied away, ran a few steps, and turned around. Jose dismounted and walked parallel to the horse's step. Whenever the horse stopped, Jose stopped too. He noticed he could get closer every time he made the right moves. Soon he could brush the horse's neck.

Jose learned that the Sommers family was from Kansas City and had bought the ranch two years before. They came with the plan to make a real success of this ranch and then return to the big city. But they didn't know a lot about rural living or just how tough it could be during cold weather. Guy had bought a few young beef cattle and let them roam on the open range. He intended to sell them once they were bigger and in good shape.

One day in November, Sommers told Jose that they needed to check on his beef cattle. Jose thought about the trips he had made with Pancho and Albert. He also remembered having to spend that awful night outdoors alone with his two goats. So he took his rifle, a few shells, an extra blanket, a machete, and a whip like Albert had used.

They rode about four hours, first north and then west. There were no cattle to be seen, but they kept going and investigated the small valleys and clumps of trees where the animals might be hidden.

The sun began to set, and Sommers suggested that they look for a place to spend the night. They found a spot that offered some protection from the wind. After tethering the horses nearby, they lay down and both were soon asleep.

The next day, they saw several animals that belonged to Sommers. They bunched them together with the intention of driving them near the ranch buildings, but four were missing from the herd. They all looked well fed, but Sommers was concerned about the possibility of a severe winter ahead. He felt like some of them might not survive.

The two men got the herd moving in the right direction. Jose's horse helped to keep them all together if some bolted away from the others. The horsemen left the animals in a place of adequate grass not far from the ranch house. Guy needed to find the four head of cattle that were missing or his profit would not equal his investment for the year.

"I'll go look for them," said Jose.

He took some food along and started off in another direction. Watching for signs, tracks, dung, or other evidence that would suggest that the cattle had been there, he rode all day. He angled back whenever necessary in order to view the whole area.

Toward nightfall, Jose discovered a stream of water that flowed southward, and it had an abundance of grass near it. He decided to spend the night and explore along the stream the next day. During the night coyotes could be heard howling nearby, but he was too tired to pay them much attention.

The next morning, he was up at dawn and could hear some cattle not far away. Because the air was still, sounds carried a long distance. He found the four cattle and got them started. Jose's horse did most of the work needed to keep them together.

Arriving home late, he told Sommers that he had left the four cattle with the first bunch.

Those critters are likely to drift off again, Sommers thought. *I wish I had a fenced area for them.*

GOD AND JESUS

Jose trained other horses to be sold. The bronco was getting accustomed to him and showed no fear. He put a blanket on its back and cinched it tightly. Speaking to the horse softly, he noted any little sign of fight or flight, and he dealt with it right away. Wild Honey was an appropriate name for the horse. It was a magnificent animal, and now that it could be ridden safely, it would fetch Sommers a good price.

"Where did you get Wild Honey?" Jose asked Guy.

"A man practically gave him to me. He wanted to get rid of him because he was so mean and terrifying. I think that horse may have a devil inside."

"It probably had a horrible time when it was branded," commented Jose. "Wild Honey has never forgotten that and has been full of fear ever since."

Surprised, Sommers asked, "How do you know it was branded?"

"You can tell it when you brush his hip on the left side. I can even see how they did it. They probably choked it, trying to get it close enough to tie its four legs together. While Wild Honey was lying on his side and struggling to get up, they put a red-hot iron on it. It must have hurt like fire. He has calmed down a lot and now shows no fear of me."

"Amazing," commented Sommers, only half-believing what he had just heard. "If you can tame that bronco, he's yours."

The following Sunday, Jose rode to church. He had never been to a church like this one and didn't know what they did or how he should act. When he arrived, the parson greeted him warmly.

"Welcome, stranger," he began. "Are you new to these parts?"

"Yes. I work for Guy Sommers."

Four or five other ranchers had come in buggies or wagons, and their children outnumbered the adults. The service started with a hymn that Jose had never heard before. Then they read from the back of the hymnal. It was a passage that Jose had read before, but he couldn't remember where. The prayer by the parson included thanks to God for His goodness and mercy. Next, the parson prayed for various people's prayer requests. Some in the church had family who were sick, and others needed ranch hands but couldn't find them. The message was from one of the Gospels. Jose couldn't forget one sentence that the parson had said: "Some of you can tame a wild horse but you can't tame your own self." He wondered what that meant.

At the end of the service the parson's wife gave some announcements, including an invitation for all to join in a dinner the following Sunday. She told them to tell their neighbors to come as well. Jose looked around and saw only two or three people who were near his age. He drifted toward the door, and a young girl came up to him, offered her hand, and told him she was glad to see him.

The next week the weather turned much colder all of a sudden, and the horses tended to stand next to any shed or bank of dirt to be protected from the wind. Jack and Jennifer talked about making a snowman. Jose had never seen snow before, so he became excited also.

The temperature dropped swiftly and plants froze, locking them in a dark night until the sun warmed the earth again in the spring. Jose saw that the bronco had no protection from the cold. He decided he would bring him to the open shed where his own horse was. He put a halter on him and led him out of the pen to the ranch house. Sommers watched him, marveling.

What can't that boy do? he thought.

The following Sunday, Jose invited the Sommers family to go to church with him. Guy declined, but his wife, eager to talk to other women, accepted readily. The children were excited because Jose had told them that other children would be at church.

When they arrived, several families were putting food in a room off to one side. During the service, the parson introduced his daughter, Kayla, who played the old pump organ and sang lustily. The message was all about God's Son, Jesus, and at the close of the service, the parson's wife invited everyone to stay for dinner. They all ate heartily, and afterward the adults began talking together in groups of three or four. The ladies helped Mrs. Sommers to feel at home, and the children both made friends quickly and enjoyed themselves. Kayla told Jack and Jennifer about the children's activities in the church. To Jose she said, "I'm so glad you came. Call me Kayla. And your name?"

"Jose Chavez. I work for the Sommerses, who live west of here."

Jose had many questions he wanted to ask somebody. The church served communion each Sunday, and he didn't understand what that was all about. He would ask the parson if he got a chance.

When they returned home, the children told their father all about the service. It became obvious to everybody that they wanted to go back to church the following Sunday. But on Saturday, it snowed and snowed and snowed. It piled into drifts and became hard due to the cold—so hard that you could walk on it. Jose, Jack, and Jennifer had a great time throwing snowballs and building a snowman as the snow began to melt and became softer.

Sommers voiced his concern about his cattle to Jose. "Do you think they have enough to eat and water to drink?" The horses pawed away snow from any grass they could find. Fortunately, in West Texas, not many days were like this one.

Christmas was now only two weeks away. At church the congregation planned another meal together, after which they planned to decorate the inside of the church. Some brought fresh branches from the evergreen trees, and some strung popcorn. Colorful gold and silver ropes and different colored balls were hung on the tree. To finish it off, candleholders with red, green, and white candles were clipped on the tree branches and would be lit during the Christmas Day service. Some of the children were learning songs and poems to present at the service.

A cheery, warm feeling was in the air everywhere as greetings were exchanged in town and at church. Before the big day arrived, the Sommerses made a trip to Big Spring. They invited Jose to ride with them in the buggy, but he declined because he wanted to ride one of the saddle horses and give it more training.

While in town, Jose bought himself a warm jacket and socks. He also took his books back to the library and chose new ones to take home with him. Noticing a newspaper on a table there, he glanced at the headline. It immediately caught his attention: "Desperado Killed in Shootout with Rangers." He continued to read and found out that Burl had died while resisting arrest. Two of his companions were taken to prison. A certain man, Francisco Cruz, who had led the rangers to the hideout, was severely wounded and died a week later.

Jose's heart just stopped! His throat became taut and dry, and he had to sit down. Pancho was dead. He could hardly believe it and cried in silence for a time. He decided to go see the marshal and get his confirmation as to just what happened.

The marshal recognized him right away and listened as Jose recounted what he had read.

"It's true," the marshal said. "I'm so sorry to hear about your friend. By the way, before he died, he said that any reward should go to you."

"I don't want the money. Give it to the poor, the widows, and those who have no homes or food so that they may have a better Christmas."

Jose went to a store and bought a little gift for Jack and Jennifer. He ran to the post office to see if there was a letter for him, but there was none.

The long ride home passed like a blur in his mind. Sobbing and crying from sadness, he shouted to no one in the cold air as he gave vent to the terrible ache he felt in his heart. He was glad to be alone but wished that Paula could have been there to console him. He thought about what Pancho had said. Had Pancho known that he would never see him again and that he would lose his life?

The words returned to his mind: "*If I don't come back, you know where I am.*"

Nothing could ease Jose's pain. He recalled again that when his mother and sister perished in the flood, he felt the same ache inside. At the ranch, a profound sadness engulfed him, and he awoke after only two or three hours of sleep. The question he wanted to ask God came up even stronger: "Why do good people like Pancho have to suffer tragedy?"

On Christmas, the Sommerses and Jose went to church. After reading the Christmas story from the Gospel of Luke, the parson gave a brief message about why Jesus came and what that should mean in each person's life. Everybody sang, and the children recited their poems.

The parson noticed that some of the candles were burning close to the bottom, so he closed the meeting with a prayer for God's blessings on the meal about to be served.

As Jose, Jack, and Jennifer were eating, Kayla came by and said to them, "Merry Christmas. I made some gingerbread cookies that I hope you like." They were delicious and everybody enjoyed them.

Jose gave his gifts to the two children after church, and they really seemed to like them. One of them was a game, and they all played it until they tired of it.

Guy showed more and more worry in his face as the days passed. His counting on the cattle to bring him some needed cash had not worked out. He lost some of them during the cold winter months, and when he took the other animals to market, there were so many cattle for sale that the price was not good. He told Mrs. Sommers that they just might have to return to Kansas City soon.

The horses Jose had worked with looked great, and they were very dependable. Those that Sommers had sold gave him some optimism and hope that there would be better days ahead.

The day came when Jose felt the bronco was ready to ride. He prepared Wild Honey, gradually introducing him to the saddle and other riding equipment that would be necessary for the horse to be ridden. The horse accepted every new thing with trust, but Jose didn't know if a rider on its back would cause him to revert to his old ways. Bucking, jumping, twisting, and trying to throw the rider was Wild Honey's former modus operandi.

Jose bridled and saddled Wild Honey and led him out to the yard, where there was an open space free of trees and bushes. He led the horse to a place where he was able to stand above the ground level and put his foot in the stirrup. Wild Honey showed no fear or apprehension, and Jose slipped into the saddle. When the horse looked around, Jose urged it ahead. He felt an unusual power under him—as though the horse could conquer the world.

One day in June, Guy announced that he was quitting ranching. He planned to sell off all his animals and put the ranch up for sale. Soon thereafter, a nicely dressed man came to the ranch. He drove a buggy that was one of the best, and his horse was big and fast. Having heard about Wild Honey, he asked to see him. Sommers showed him to the man, and he asked if the horse was for sale.

"You'll have to ask my helper. His name is Jose, and it's his horse."

The man called to Jose, and he appeared from the shed, where he had been trimming the hooves of some of the horses.

"Son, would you like to sell me that horse? I want to have a closer look at him and watch somebody ride him."

Jose then turned to Sommers. "He's your horse. Sell him if you like."

"Saddle the horse and ride him for us, Jose," exclaimed Guy.

"It's a beautiful horse," the visitor commented. "Tell me what you want for him."

"The only person who has ever ridden that horse is the young man you see now," replied Sommers. "He has not been broken to pull a buggy or run in races. I think I should tell you that."

"That's fine. Now give me a price."

Sommers thought for a brief moment. "How about one hundred dollars?"

"That's too much for any horse out here," said the man irritably.

Jose took Wild Honey away. After a few minutes, the man wanted to see the horse again and went into the shed where it stayed. Jose wasn't there, and the horse reverted to its old ways— screaming and kicking its hind legs up in the air. The man, afraid to get near him, got into his buggy, slapped his horse with the reins, and rode away quickly.

That night Jose told his boss that he would like to take Wild Honey to Big Spring to see how he would react to new noises and different situations. The horse would have to be tried in that way before being sold.

The day came, and Jose put on his best clothes. He put the nicest saddle on Wild Honey. Because the horse had a long stride, he made the trip into town in record time. Jose rode up and down the streets where people noticed him and admired the beautiful horse. Strange noises were no problem, but when Jose tied him briefly to go into a store, the horse became anxious. He stamped his front feet like a defiant child. Jose picked up the reins and was ready to ride off, but the man who had visited the ranch approached him.

"I watched you ride into town," he said. "The horse is not afraid of either noises or people. I still want to buy it."

"You'll have to talk to Sommers about that," said Jose. "If it were my horse, it would come in first in this summer's parade, and it would take first prize." As he rode away, he felt proud to be riding Wild Honey.

As the summer wore on, there was less and less work for Jose to do. He got out his knife and began a carving that he planned to enter in the county fair at Big Spring. He found a block of wood that had a blond streak running lengthwise. It would be great if he could make a horse's head with that blaze of color coming down its face from forehead to nose. He used Wild Honey as his model, and in a few days he had an exact replica of the horse. The neck suggested power and strength.

Jose had put forth his best effort into this carving in the hopes that he would get a prize. He carved his name underneath the piece as the deadline neared for submitting items in the craft section. He got his carving in on time and continued the ranch work as usual.

"Jose, as much as I hate it, I will have to let you go at the end of July," Sommers told him. "Please feel free to begin looking for more work. We have enjoyed having you, and you have become a friend to my family and me."

Jose felt sad that the Sommers family dreams were ending like this.

He went to church on the Sunday before he left the Sommerses and bade farewell to those whom he had come to know. He told them he was out of work and would probably be going on to Lubbock.

Kayla looked disappointed and asked, "Will you be going to the fair?"

"Sure," said Jose. "I entered a carving that I did of my horse."

"I have entered an embroidered tablecloth," Kayla volunteered.

"Maybe I'll see you there," Jose told her. "I'll treat you to a cup of hot chocolate."

When it came time to say good-bye to the parson, Jose told him he had many questions he would like to ask him. The parson invited Jose to his house, where they could have a long talk.

The fair began the next day. Crowds of people watched the parade of horses, buggies, bicycles, and bands from various places. They all displayed their banners. Jose went over to the craft section to check on his carving. He found the sewing and embroidery and looked at it also. As he looked, Kayla came up and showed him what she had done. The white tablecloth had beautiful embroidered flowers on it, and they were in colors of blue, green, and yellow. The cloth was trimmed with lace.

"It's very pretty," said Jose. "I hope you get first prize."

"I want to see your carving," Kayla said.

He showed her where the carvings were, and she looked for his name. He had to point it out to her.

"It's beautiful. How did you do it?" exclaimed Kayla.

"Well," answered Jose, "on this particular piece it became obvious that I needed to follow my heart when I carved it. I felt strongly that Wild Honey should be my model."

Looking a bit embarrassed, Jose tried to cover it. "What kind of animal do you like? I'll make one for you."

"I like cougars. They are the prettiest animals in the world."

"You mean pumas, don't you?" Jose teased.

"No, I mean mountain lions," she retorted. They both laughed.

The judging would be the next day, and they would know how their entries had fared. Jose spent the rest of the day looking at the finest animals in the county. There were all sorts of cattle, horses, pigs, chickens, ducks, turkeys, and rabbits.

The next day, there was an even bigger crowd of people than the day before. The judges of the sewing, bakery items, canning, vegetables, corn, cotton, and many other things were deciding on the best entries. They gave blue ribbons for first prize, red ribbons for second, and white ribbons for third prizes. Jose watched Kayla observing the judges. She received a first prize.

"Congratulations," said Jose warmly. "Would you like your cup of hot chocolate now?"

"Sure. And thanks."

Her smile is beautiful, thought Jose. They looked for a place where coffee and hot chocolate were served, and the two sat at a small table and chatted for a while.

"What will you do now, Jose?" Kayla asked.

"I don't know. I may go to Lubbock to look for work, or I may go back and finish high school. Have you finished school?"

She looked sad and didn't answer directly. "My parents don't want me to go to school. My mother's health is not good, and I have to stay at home to help her."

They finished their drinks and returned to the craft section of the fair. Kayla saw it first and with a loud exclamation said, "You did it, Jose! Congratulations on your blue ribbon." They laughed together over it. With an impish smile, Kayla quipped, "I knew you would get a blue!"

A sign on the table read "Pick up your entries by Saturday."

Kayla told him she had to leave and meet her family.

Jose looked at the other things in the craft section. He wasn't aware of anyone close by until a familiar voice greeted him. "Hello, Jose."

He turned to find Elena standing behind him. "Elena, what are you doing here?"

She looked more beautiful than ever, and he wanted to hold her tightly and tell her how much he had missed her.

"I came through looking at the crafts and saw your carving. I could tell it was yours by its workmanship, so I figured you must be in the area."

"I'm so happy to see you, Elena. It's been so long." Her face showed no joy, and he wondered why.

"Who is the girl?" she asked.

"Just a friend," Jose replied. "Could we sit down somewhere and talk? I want to hear all about you. Did you get my message I sent to Paula?"

They moved to a bench outside.

"I no longer teach in Quemada," explained Elena. "I have moved to another town not far from here."

"Where's that?"

She did not reply to his question, but asked, "Where have you been during this time, and what have you been doing?"

Jose told her briefly about being held in Burl's hideout and how he and Pancho had escaped. "I got a job on a nearby ranch here, but my work was terminated recently."

"So now what are your plans?"

"Now that I have found you again, I don't know. I'll do anything to be with you."

She seemed cool to this idea, and Jose became puzzled.

"You told me you loved me," Elena said. "But you don't really know what love is."

"Really?" he said. "Love dies if it doesn't receive back. You ran away, and I never saw you again, so I felt rejected and worthless."

"Well, you didn't come to say good-bye," she reminded him.

"I have been sorry for that a thousand times. Can you forgive me?"

He saw that she had become disturbed and upset.

"What's the matter?" he asked. His voice was full of compassion and caring.

"Jose, let's just be friends. I have been married for two years now, and I have a little girl who is only a year old."

As he listened, Jose's world seemed to turn upside down. That night, he had a hard time sleeping. When he did sleep, he tossed and turned—always on the edge of waking up.

Morning finally came, but he didn't feel rested. He got up and decided to go see the parson. The two men went into a room where a few books lined the wall. A big Bible lay on a desk beside a lamp with a chimney, which had been blackened by soot. Jose sat down, not knowing where to start.

Pancho's death still stirred frequently in his heart. He asked this man whom he respected, "Why do innocent and good people die in tragedies, and why is it that I always seem to lose those who are the dearest to me?" Jose told the minister about his past life.

"I cannot tell you the answer to your question," replied the parson. "But there are many things that I don't understand either. In your case, you can be thankful that you were not home on that awful night the storm erased your house. All I can say for sure is that God is good and He is in control. And another thing comes to mind, now that I think about it. Through our difficulties, losses, and trials, God is teaching us many important lessons. Perhaps the most important lesson is that we need to always give him praise, no matter what our circumstances are. These lessons help us to mature and grow spiritually."

"Tell me why the sign at the church says 'Christian Church,' and what does that mean?"

"When the pioneers came west, many of them had belonged to various churches that had different names. There were not very many who belonged to the same group; that is to say, they couldn't survive as a church with so few members. Therefore, folks got together and decided they would call themselves the Christian Church.

"Members are expected to believe in the teachings of the Holy Scriptures, make a profession of faith in Christ, and be baptized.

You might ask, what is a Christian? To me, a Christian is one who has made a choice to follow Jesus Christ and honor and hold Him above anything else. The Christian is one who has left his old ways and sins and, through God's Spirit, lives a new life. As the Apostle Paul teaches us, the Christian is a new person."

"What should I be concerned with most then?" asked Jose.

The parson looked at him with genuine love before he spoke. "The thing you need to do is to make your personal decision to follow Jesus, to open your life to him, and let him be your boss. Seek God's will in all you do. Remember this verse: 'Trust in the Lord with all your heart and lean not on your own understanding; in all your ways acknowledge him and he will make your paths straight' (Proverbs 3:5-6, NIV). Christ saves us through His grace, and that was what happened when he died on the cross for all our sins.

"Let me suggest something that will be even more helpful to you, Jose. Each morning after you get up, find a quiet place to read something from the Bible. Then give God praise and glory for all He does. Pray for your needs, as well as those around you. Give thanks and then keep a record of how God answers you."

He put his hand on Jose's shoulder and prayed. "May the Lord bless and keep you always."

Jose listened intently. He thought he understood, and some questions had been answered. He and the parson said good-bye, closing another chapter in Jose's young life. He headed for Lubbock. One deep regret that remained in his heart was that he had left Wild Honey, the horse among horses. Would he ever see the horse again, and would his next owner treat him right?

HORSE RACES

Jose went by the employment office once more before leaving Big Spring. He saw an AD for a ranch hand on the outskirts of town, and the AD was signed "Dr. Alejandro Luna." The mile or more of tree-lined streets leading out of town were unpaved, and one saw only an occasional house.

Upon arriving at the gate of the ranch, Jose noticed two horses grazing beside the road. The house was of simple design and had several rooms, but the large screen porch, which surrounded it on three sides, was its most beautiful trait.

After tying his horse to a post, Jose knocked on the door, and a middle-aged woman with flour-covered arms opened the door. Obviously she had been baking. Looking Jose up and down, she asked him what he wanted.

"Is Dr. Luna here?" he asked. "I saw an AD in town that said he was looking for a ranch hand, and I'm looking for work."

"He won't be in until late afternoon," she replied. "But if you will bring me some wood for the stove and water from the well, I'll give you something to eat."

Jose did as she asked and sat down to a delicious meal. He was used to eating in silence, but this woman kept asking him questions: "Where were you born? Have you finished school? Where did you last work?" Jose answered politely but gave few details.

Then she said, "There was a man who worked here before, but he had to leave recently due to his poor health."

Since Jose had to wait to see Dr. Luna, he thanked the woman for the meal and offered to help her with some chores. After these were done, he moved his horse to a place where there was some grass along the roadside. He then went to the corral, where he had seen two horses. Entering the corral, he approached the first horse. It kept eating grass, paying no attention to him. The second horse, showing alarm and fear, wouldn't let him come close at all, and Jose wondered why. It was a young horse and may not have been broken to ride yet. He could not help but compare this horse to Wild Honey. Upon moving close to a buggy parked nearby, he noticed a well-worn harness hanging on the wall inside the barn. Also, there were several horse stalls and a pen where others could be kept. A large tank of water was full, and a windmill stood a few feet away, although it wasn't pumping any water. The occasional gust of wind made the windmill rattle and creak.

Finally, Dr. Luna arrived. He had walked from his office in town since he always enjoyed walking. He was about the same height as Jose but considerably heavier. The slight graying of his hair and the lines in his face showed him to be middle age.

Greeting Jose warmly, he said, "Will you excuse me please? Just sit down on the porch and make yourself comfortable."

When Dr. Luna returned, and after having talked to the cook, he knew why Jose was there. "So you are looking for work," he began as he scrutinized Jose. "I need somebody to tend my horses and do some chores around these buildings. You know, I am a doctor, and sometimes I have to visit patients out in the country. So one of your chores would be to hitch up the horse to the buggy and drive me wherever I need to go. It usually doesn't take long, but the hour can be inconvenient."

"Well, I don't mind," Jose assured him.

"I have some quarter horses about a mile from here, and I keep them for racing. That's my vice. Sometimes I make money, and sometimes I lose it, but racing keeps me busy and out of mischief. Come with me and I'll show you which horse goes with the buggy. You may put your horse in the corral."

They went down to the fenced-in area. The doctor explained that the one horse was not broken to ride but the other was gentle and would give Jose no problem.

"Tomorrow we'll go to see the other horses since you will be spending lots of time with them. I need to get a couple of them ready for the upcoming races."

The two men went back to the house. It was suppertime, and the table was set for three. Jose heard Dr. Luna call the cook Jenny, and she called him Alejandro. They all talked freely, and Jose enjoyed the family-like atmosphere. Both of them asked more questions of Jose and urged him to tell them his story.

"I'm an orphan," he began. "My mother and little sister were washed away in a great flood of the Rio Grande River. Some kind people took me in, and I finished two years of high school. Since then, I have been on my own."

"Where have you worked recently?" the doctor asked.

"At Guy Sommers's ranch west of here. He just retired from ranching and plans to return to Kansas City."

Dr. Luna appeared to be listening intently and seemed interested in Jose's story. He had heard of Sommers and his horses. He had also heard about a big gray horse that struck fear in the hearts of tough cowboys.

"Tell me about the mean bronco that Mr. Sommers owns. I believe that any horse can be broken to ride. You just have to break their spirit by force. I want to see that horse sometime."

The next day, the two men rode out to where the quarter horses were kept. They were fine-looking animals and appeared to have been well cared for. Dr. Luna told Jose about each horse and praised one in particular for having won some important races.

Every day the horses were given a good workout in the large, open space that resembled a racetrack. Dr. Luna invited Jose to ride one of them.

"I know nothing about racing," Jose told him, but he mounted and let the horse choose his pace. When he leaned forward in the saddle, the horse took off on a fast gallop. Pure pleasure possessed Jose, and he was hooked on racing.

The following day, he cleaned the barn, repaired some broken straps, and brushed down the horses. The young horse gave him some trouble when he tried to put a halter on it. It had rolled in the dirt many times, and its hide was full of dust and stickers.

Riding to where the quarter horses were kept, Jose immediately noticed that one of the horses walked with a limp. Cautiously, he moved beside the horse and lifted the lame foot. Placing the horse's foot on his knee, he examined the bottom of the hoof. Jose saw nothing wrong with it, but he probed each area of the hoof until the horse tended to pull away when it hurt.

Then he took out his knife and cut away some of the excess growth. Underneath the stained, yellowish, spongy growth was a white, healthy base. Cutting deeper would mean touching nerve tissue, and the horse wouldn't stand for that. Jose put pressure on different parts of the exposed area, and again the horse tried to pull away. He looked more carefully at the spot and noticed a small fissure in which a piece of sharp glass had penetrated the hoof. Releasing the foot, he let the horse stand on it. After a few minutes, he raised it again and pried the glass out. He put it away to show to Dr. Luna later. Then he gave each of the horses a workout, including a fast run around the racetrack.

He didn't notice the young girl who had climbed the rail fence and was sitting on top. When he returned to the stables, he saw her. She had no cap on, and her hair was short with tight curls clinging to her scalp. She wore boys' overalls and a plaid shirt, and he guessed her age to be about twelve or thirteen.

"Who are you?" she asked. Her freckle-covered face broke out in a friendly smile.

"Name's Jose," he told her. "What's your name, and what brings you here?"

"I like to watch horses, and I used to come down here when the other man came to tend to them. I know the names of every one and can tell you which have won races. Have you ever won a horse race?"

"No, I have never raced horses, but maybe I will someday. You haven't told me your name."

"My name is Natalie, and you can call me Nat, like everyone else does. I live with my mother in the next house down the road."

"Well, Nat, what's your mother's name?"

"Nellie. When I was born, she wanted a boy, and she tries to treat me like one by cutting my hair short and not allowing me to wear dresses. I can run as fast as any boy and throw a ball just as well. But I'm a girl! Do you suppose girls could ever ride in horse races?"

"Don't you go to school?" continued Jose.

"I go when I want to, but the boys make fun of me because I don't wear dresses. They also talk about my hair, laugh at my clothes, and mock me because I don't have a father."

"Look, Nat, I'm sorry about your father, but I don't have a father or a mother. And sure, you can learn to ride a horse and race. Why not? Do you know Jenny, the cook? We'll see if we can get you some dresses and girl stuff, okay?"

"Would you?" she exclaimed. Jose saw hope and anticipation cover her face, and her dark eyes danced with pleasure. She scrambled down from the top of the corral and disappeared in an instant. That night at suppertime, before Dr. Luna arrived, Jose asked Jenny about Nat.

"So you have met her. We call her Nat, but I think her name should be 'gnat.' She is such a pest—always showing up when you don't want her to. And no one can ask more questions than she can! So what did you learn about her?"

"She says her mother wanted a boy and now treats her like one. Also, she told me she has no dresses to wear. Is that true? Has she got any friends? And what does her mother do? Do they live alone, just the two of them?" Now it was Jose's time to ask the questions.

Jenny loved to talk, but there were few people to talk to since she spent most of her time on the ranch. The times she hitched the horse to the buggy to go to town were times when she was able to socialize with the other women. Jenny's trips to town usually lasted several hours since she also had to do her grocery shopping. She began telling Jose about Nat's mother.

"She was married to a man who left her for reasons I don't know. Perhaps he was not ready to accept the responsibility of being a father, but Nat was born three months after he abandoned her mother, so she never knew him. It's too bad because all girls need a father's guiding influence in their lives. It's true that her mother doesn't treat her very well and she will sometimes whip Nat with a belt when she doesn't go to school. I have seen her staring in the glass windows of stores where there are children's dresses and girls' things. One time she came here crying because her mother cut off all her hair and made her look like a boy. The boys in town tease her about her freckles and curly hair. She didn't pass into the next grade last year because she missed so much school."

"What can we do to help?" asked Jose. His heart was deeply moved because he thought of his own little sister, who would have been about Nat's age. He could imagine her going through some of the same problems that Nat had faced.

"Would you do me a favor, Jenny? If I give you the money, could you buy some girls' clothes for Nat? Help her fix her hair—see if you can flatten those curls—and buy her a pretty bonnet to wear. We'll go together with Nat to present her to her mother. How does that sound to you?"

"I'm just not sure," said Jenny. "I'll be glad to get some clothes, and then we can have a party here and invite her mother to come. That way she won't explode in anger when she sees Nat all dressed up. And then you can take them both home in the buggy."

The next day, Dr. Luna took the buggy without saying where he was going. Jose did the usual things around the barn and house, and then he rode to the stables. He observed Nat looking miserable and sitting on the top rung of the corral with her head in her hands. She heard Jose arrive but gave him only a halfhearted greeting.

"Cheer up, young lady," Jose remarked. "Get ready to ride. If you're going to be a girl today, you better begin now."

Nat looked totally bewildered. Had she already forgotten their conversation of a day or two ago? Jose told her how to get into the saddle. She couldn't reach the stirrup in which to put her foot. Leading the horse so she could stand on a little stool, Jose put her foot in the stirrup while she grabbed the horn and swung her other leg over the horse. Her feet didn't reach low enough, so she placed them in the straps that were above the stirrups.

"Are you afraid?" he asked her. "This horse is gentle and won't buck you off, so don't worry. To stop, you just pull back on the reins."

"You go with me," Nat pleaded in a weak voice.

With a great leap and pull at the saddle, Jose mounted and was sitting in back of Nat. He sensed the apprehension in her body. Jose told Nat he was dismounting. He began brushing and currying the other horses as Nat continued her ride.

When Nat returned to where she started, her face showed pure delight. She smiled and showed a perfect set of teeth and a small dimple in each cheek. Sliding off of the horse, she patted it on the neck.

"Congratulations!" said Jose.

"Thanks to you," said Nat clearly.

"Why did you look so glum when I got here?"

"My mother says I shouldn't come here," she replied. "I told her about you and that you were now working for Dr. Luna. She told me to stay away and avoid trouble."

"I want to meet your mother, Nat. Just continue to obey her, and we'll work something out so you can learn to ride."

Nat left and Jose finished his work. He arrived home just in time to see Dr. Luna enter the driveway. Behind the buggy was Wild Honey. He was wearing a sturdy halter, and it was tied to a strong lariat. Jose was shocked to see that his friend had been badly mistreated. There was blood dripping from the horse's nose where the halter had worn into his skin. Wild Honey was trembling with fear.

Dr. Luna looked stern and angry. When the buggy stopped in front of the barn, Wild Honey jerked his head up and pulled back violently. Unable to do anything else, he reared his hind legs into the air while uttering a sharp warning. Jose hurried to calm the horse down.

He said to Dr. Luna, "Just leave him to me, and I'll take care of everything."

Cautiously, Jose approached Wild Honey while talking soothingly to him. Wild Honey recognized Jose's voice and waited. After untying the lariat from the buggy, he urged the horse forward. The wheels had made horrible grinding noises as they bounced over the gravel road for the past several hours. Jose patted Wild Honey's neck and talked to him as though he understood.

"You don't have to be afraid now. You have come home, and we're back together. Let me see how your nose is."

Jose carefully lifted the strap from the front of the horse's nose and wrapped some cloth bands around the strap so it would give space between the sore and the strap. That way it no longer irritated the area. He would have liked to take the halter off, but he was sure Dr. Luna wouldn't like that. So he led the horse to a separate corral and let him loose. Dr. Luna observed all of this with amazement. Then he went inside the house.

Jose noticed that Dr. Luna was visibly shaken. The doctor volunteered information about his trip. "I didn't know if I would get here in one piece or not," he said. "That horse kept me in a tug-of-war for most of the way. What did you do to calm him down?"

"He is a one-man horse," replied Jose. "I treat him as I would a special person. He trusts me completely and knows that I wouldn't harm or injure him in any way. He doesn't have that trust for others, and I think I know why. How did you get him?"

"Sommers was glad to sell Wild Honey. He told me about the difficulty everyone had in working with him and that none of the ranchers nearby cared to risk their lives trying to tame him. I paid only twenty-five dollars for that big hunk of useless horseflesh!"

"What do you plan to do with him?"

"I don't know just yet. He won't let me come near and acts like he would like to plant both hind hooves in my backside. Reminds me of a very naughty child who screams, kicks, and pulls away when angry."

Jose laughed. "I bet that horse can beat any horse in the races."

"Oh sure," Dr. Luna replied with sarcasm. "If that's true, he's worth thousands of dollars. But who could ever ride him? Perhaps he would be good for the rodeo, where the bronco busters have to stay on for twenty seconds to win any money."

Every afternoon during the weeks that followed, the doctor would ride his horses around the track. They looked great after their daily brushing. Nat came often to talk to Jose. He didn't mind, but he saw the need to challenge her to pursue a dream.

"You go to school every day and I'll let you ride my horse as much as you like after you get home. I'll even let you ride some other horse after you learn more and are not afraid. Think about it, and you can become the best girl rider in this town. It may be tough, and the boys will mock you. But if you never try it, you won't ever know what you might have been able to do."

Jose saw the determination in her face, and when she smiled, he knew she would accept the offer.

Jose never neglected Wild Honey. He checked the sores on his nose daily and saw that they were healing. The horse showed genuine gladness when Jose came to see him. In horse language, he was saying, "Get on my back and I'll give you the ride of your life!" Or so Jose thought.

At least once a week, Nat told Jose her birthday was coming up. She would be fifteen, but she looked much younger. Her hair had grown longer, and her freckles were less prominent.

"What would you like for your birthday?" Jose asked her one day.

"I never get birthday presents," she almost sobbed. "I have nothing to wear at a party, and my mother can't buy new clothes for me."

"Next Sunday morning, you come and help Jenny make cookies. Tell your mother that I will pick you up in the buggy and bring you here. You can invite some friends if you like, and we will have a party. How's that?"

Sunday came, and Nat showed up in her best overalls. She and Jenny made some cookies for the party. Then Jenny took her into her room and told her to put on the clothes that she had bought. Nat needed some coaching to put the clothes on right. She was so pleased she was speechless. After she put on the shiny black shoes, Nat could no longer contain herself.

"Are these for me?"

Jenny combed her hair and put a pretty ribbon on each side. Then she placed a bonnet on Nat's head. It covered some of her short hair and gave her the appearance of being taller. She stood before the mirror.

"Who do you see in there?" Jenny asked her. "I've never seen her before now."

With a puzzled look and in a weak voice, Nat replied, "I've never seen her before either."

When the two of them came out to the dining room, the doctor and Jose were waiting.

"Wow!" exclaimed Dr. Luna. "You're the prettiest girl in town."

Nat blushed, and Jose nodded his agreement. He left and went to get Nat's mother. A few other guests that had been invited by Dr. Luna arrived. They retired to the den to talk about the upcoming races. Owners of racehorses came from other cities, so the event became bigger and bigger each year.

When Jose got back and Nat's mother entered the house, she barely recognized her own daughter. She could hardly believe her eyes. The transformation was like the contrast of a worm changed to a butterfly when it comes out of a cocoon. Nat turned to her mother.

"Do you like my new clothes?" Nat asked, searching her mother's face for approval.

"They are very nice," her mother said, more to Jenny than to her daughter. "You must keep them clean and be careful not to tear the dress."

Nat's joy was boundless. She beamed with happiness as she asked her mother: "Can I wear dresses to school like the other girls?"

Her mother remained silent. Jenny told everyone to sit at the table, and she served them refreshments. The conversation around the room was loud, and everyone had a good time. Everybody wished Nat well, and the birthday party was a huge success.

Dr. Luna and Jose worked hard to get the horses at their best for the races. They timed the horses for the mile-and-a-quarter race. Jose wondered who the rider would be.

Dr. Luna told him, "There are jockeys who make their living by riding in the big races. They receive a percentage of any money won. They are usually small of stature and lightweight."

Quarter horse races were becoming more popular, and some of the richest purses of all horse racing involved quarter horses. Some of the horses became well known and were worth thousands of dollars.

One day Jose took Wild Honey out to the racetrack. He had never ridden the horse at his full speed, and he didn't know if

Wild Honey would refuse to be enclosed in a gate. He made a makeshift gate with a swinging door, and then he led the horse to the gate and coaxed him inside. There was no extra room in that little space, and the horse acted apprehensive. Jose talked gently and assured Wild Honey that things were all right. Nat opened the gate door, and Jose and his mount were out in a flash. The horse's strong back legs propelled them to top speed in no time. Sensing what was wanted of him, Wild Honey reached out to cover the distance as quickly as possible. They practiced going in and out of the starting gate. Jose was ready to give competition to Dr. Luna's other horses.

Nat became quite a rider; she could saddle Jose's smaller horse and make it gallop at full speed. She attended school faithfully and nearly every day after school, she was at the stables.

A week before the races began, Jose posed a challenge to his boss. "I'll race you on Wild Honey one time around the track."

"Why not? It will be good for my horse to have the experience," replied Dr. Luna.

The signal was given, and the doctor's horse shot forward and was five lengths ahead when Wild Honey responded. He ran even faster and then ran neck and neck with Dr. Luna's horse. Then Jose urged his mount to go even faster. Dr. Luna shook his head in disbelief. Wild Honey looked as if he could easily run two miles without difficulty. Dr. Luna began to think about how he could put Jose in the races, knowing that no other horse would be able to beat Wild Honey.

Rumors began to spread around town that an unknown horse would be racing. People began placing bets on horses they had seen before or on horses that had reputations for winning. The roster contained the names of the horses and the jockeys who would be riding them. As an anomaly, the roster said, "Jose Chavez on Wild Honey." The odds were forty to one. If Wild Honey won, the ticket holder would get forty dollars for every one dollar he had bet."

Hundreds of people arrived before the races began, and excitement permeated the air. Tension was high and ripe for the race. Horse owners had their jockeys dressed in colorful garb and black caps. Each of the jockeys carried a quirt. Jose wore his regular clothes and carried nothing with which to beat his horse. There were only five gates.

Fifteen horses were scheduled to race. The track, however, wasn't big enough to accommodate them all at the same time. The first race pitted one of Luna's horses against four others. The horse performed well but not well enough and didn't place in the first two spots.

The next race was to take place about an hour later, so Luna entered his second horse. During this time, Jose sat and silently observed the betting and all the other goings-on. Those who lost in the first race bet more heavily on a horse in the second race. It became an addiction for many.

Each of the five horses was called by name and was led to the starting gate. At the sound of the gates opening, the horses bounded out and quickly jockeyed for position. Toward the end of the race, the jockeys, by beating their mounts, tried to get the utmost speed out of them. Dr. Luna's horse came in second. Jose thought out his strategy for the next race and decided that he would run just fast enough to keep up with the others until the last few seconds. Then he would move ahead to win.

Dr. Luna came up to him and asked, "Are you ready? Nobody is betting on you to win. They don't know you or the horse, so I'm going to place my bet of five dollars that you will win. If the odds are the same as they have been—forty to one—I'll make two hundred dollars and you will get a fourth of that." Like many other addicts, Dr. Luna laughed, began to plan for the next races, and knew that he would probably win this one coming up.

The race was called up, and Jose led Wild Honey to the gate. He whispered something to him and placed his hand gently on the horse. This helped Wild Honey to feel assured that everything was all right.

The gate opened with a clang, and the horses all shot out of their boxes, quickly getting in the rhythm of the fast pace. Jose stayed away from the pack, but he kept up with the leaders. The crowd cheered loudly for the favorite.

Worry, however, showed on the faces of some of the horse owners who could see that the big, gray, unknown horse easily matched the others. A few yards from the finish line, Jose gave his signal to Wild Honey to stretch out and go a bit faster. He won by a half length!

The betting crowd was stunned and silent. Many of them looked bewildered, and their smiles became scowls as they held their betting tickets in their hands. The announcer barked out the race for the next day. The six horses that had come in first and second in the three races of the day would also be racing tomorrow. People were allowed to place their bets at any time until a half hour before the race.

Jose took Wild Honey home, but he didn't feel too good about the whole thing. He felt uneasy and had a foreboding about an unknown tragedy that might take place tomorrow. He led Wild Honey into the corral, and he put some whole corn in the feeding bin. That was all the reward Wild Honey would get.

After turning around, Jose saw Nat. Her face beamed, and her sparkling eyes danced with pride.

"I saw you ride and win on Wild Honey today," she exclaimed. "My mother and I went to the races. Weren't they exciting?"

"How are things with your mother?"

"She is different ever since the party. Now we can talk together and have fun. She lets me wear dresses to school, and my hair is growing out."

"That's good," Jose commented. "I'm so happy for you."

Nat left and Jose retired to a quiet spot to think. Why did he feel so unsettled and worried about tomorrow? Would something else happen to him? These questions tugged at him.

Dr. Luna had been looking for Jose and found him sitting on a low box in the barn.

"You performed well today," he said. "Here's the fifty dollars that you earned. There will be a bigger purse tomorrow."

"Keep the money," Jose told him. "I don't like to make money like that. And the only reason I am going to ride again tomorrow is to show that Wild Honey is the best horse around here. It's the horse that should get the prize."

"Well, I'll keep the money for you until later," replied the doctor.

The next day, the six horses were there. Luna pulled his horse from the race at the last minute since there were only five gates to accommodate the horses. The doctor knew that Wild Honey would win anyway. The hawkers who took bets called out their odds, and the announcer made it known that there would be only one winner. The first horse to arrive at the finish line would take the whole purse. People placed their bets and sat down to wait.

The jockeys, looking at Jose and Wild Honey, did not smile. There was something sinister in their actions. One of them took Jose aside and said, "I'll give you fifty dollars if you will blow the race."

"What do you mean?" asked Jose.

"You can hold back or make your horse stumble, or something like that. Just don't win!"

Anger arose in Jose. *So that's what goes on in races*, he thought.

Nat and her mother came by to wish Jose well, and they told him that they were betting ten dollars on Wild Honey. The odds were announced on each of the five horses, and Wild Honey was twenty-five to one.

The horses were called up, and Jose went into the outside gate.

"You have to come through for me now," he whispered to Wild Honey. "Not to make money for me or anybody else, but I want you to show that you are the best horse here."

The gates swung open, and the horses shot out of their little cages. Jose didn't hold back at all this time. Before he and Wild Honey came to the first turn, they were several lengths ahead of the others. He kept urging Wild Honey to go faster, and they crossed the finish line in record time. The other horses pounded across half a minute later. There was anger and pandemonium in the stands. Some people were yelling, "Foul!" and others were demanding that the race be nullified. Horse owners had lost a lot of money, and they knew that if Wild Honey was to be on the racing circuit, they would lose even more.

Luna had bet heavily on Wild Honey, so he collected a good sum of money. When he got home, Jose was already there, but he wasn't happy. Jose was thinking that maybe he should leave town.

Dr. Luna approached him. "That was a spectacular win for you today. Did you see those two guys in dark suits, shirts, and ties? They were the owners of the horses everyone expected to win. When it was all over, they came up to me and asked me if I would sell Wild Honey. I told them no, and they got so mad! They are just not used to losing races or losing money. I sure don't trust them in the future races, and I would be extremely careful if I were you."

Jose remained silent. He thoughtfully reviewed the race events, and then he decided not to mention the fact that a jockey had offered him money if he would deliberately lose the race.

He spoke with a clear and definite voice, "My days of racing are over."

Dr. Luna's voice showed surprise. "But why? You can make a lot of money if you continue to race like you did today."

"I just don't like it," Jose declared. "So don't plan on me ever riding again."

"Think about it for a while. Perhaps you will change your mind," said the doctor as he went inside the house.

Jose checked all the animals to see that they had plenty to eat and enough water to drink. He spent extra time with Wild Honey, telling him what a great horse he was and that he was his best friend. He hugged the horse, patted him on the neck, and scratched behind his ears.

That evening at the supper table, the conversation was strangely different. Jenny tried to find out how the races went, but neither man made much conversation about them. Jose went to his room and lay down on the bed. He wasn't sleepy, and he felt a deep restlessness in his heart that he could not explain. As he thought about his past, he remembered all of his losses: his mother and Angelica, Paula, Pancho, and several others. He became depressed and grief-stricken once again. Paula did not die, but Jose lost her when he left home. The question that he had always asked came to mind, haunting him once again: *Why isn't God helping me, or why isn't he on my side? Will these tragedies never end?*

ANOTHER DEATH

Jose awoke early the next morning while it was still dark. The house was silent, and even the chickens were still roosting on low branches in the trees. All of a sudden, a shot rang out in the distance. It was followed by a strange noise, which sounded like the fearful sound of a frightened animal. He got up and dressed. When he opened the door, he heard the sound of hoof beats as a horse galloped away in the distance. He went to the barn, where everything seemed to be normal. Stopping to listen, he heard the sound of escaping air. The sound was repeated but softer, and finally it stopped.

Jose climbed the fence and went to look for Wild Honey. He called out, but there was no response. Climbing a small knoll, he peered into the shadows made by some trees. There on the ground lay Wild Honey. He was dead—shot by a despicable coward.

Jose ran to where the horse lay and could not believe what he saw. He knelt down and tried to speak just as he used to do, but words would not come. Tears welled up in his eyes, and he wanted to strike out at the nearest object. He became indescribably angry. He stroked Wild Honey's head and neck as tenderly as one would do to console a child. Then he sat down beside his horse, leaned his head on him, and closed his eyes. His dark world became even darker, and he began to cry.

Daybreak melded into the light of dawn. Dr. Luna had his breakfast and prepared to return to his practice. He wanted to talk to Jose and give him some instructions, but Jose was nowhere within calling distance. After looking around for some time, he decided to check on Wild Honey. Going into the pasture, he walked toward the same hill that Jose had climbed a couple of hours earlier. What he saw astounded him. He approached the grieving boy and his dead horse with caution.

"What happened?" the doctor said in a soft voice.

Jose raised his tear-stained face away from the sound of the doctor's voice. Words would hardly come, but suddenly he blurted out, "Somebody shot Wild Honey!"

"Come away," the doctor said after a few minutes. "There is nothing you can do here now. Take the day off and I'll see that the horse is buried."

The two men walked back toward the house, and Jose said, "I awoke in the middle of the night, and after a while, I heard a rifle shot. I went outside and could hear the sound of fast hoof beats in the distance."

After their return to the house, Jenny asked, "Would you like some breakfast, Jose?"

"Thanks, but I'm not hungry."

He tried to relax, but thoughts kept piling up in his mind. *Who would do a thing like this? And what future is there in staying here any longer? Is there some balm for the ache in my heart or some solace for the pain in my soul? Is there something I have done to displease God?*

He wished Pancho were here. He would know what to do. Jose tried to imagine what Pancho would have said, and then he remembered Pancho's words to him about the Bible: "*If you ever need help, just read that little book and pray.*"

Jose had not paid attention to that little book in quite some time. He looked for it under several things he had accumulated since coming to work here. Then he opened it and selected this passage to read: "Cast all your anxiety on him because he cares for you" (1 Peter 5:7, NIV).

As he looked at the top of the page, he discovered that the disciple Peter had written these words. Then he remembered the story he had heard about the disciples caught in a bad storm on a lake. They had been about to sink in the water and became really alarmed because Jesus was sound asleep in the boat. After he awakened, Jesus spoke to the winds and the water. Then suddenly everything was quiet, and a great calm descended on them.

Do you suppose Jesus could calm the pain in my heart? Jose thought.

He could almost hear Pancho saying: "*Just ask Him.*"

He closed his eyes and said, "I don't know much about praying, but I feel so bad. My best friend was shot, and now I'm alone. Can you soothe the ache in my heart? I am asking for your help and peace, God."

After reading some more in the book of Peter and some other passages, Jose felt better. He decided he would go check on the horses in the stables. He performed his usual duties there and brushed and checked on all of them. He decided to skip dinner since he had found some relief in keeping busy.

About four o'clock Nat arrived, dressed in faded overalls and scrubby shoes. She said, "I heard Wild Honey was shot last night. I bet you must feel awfully bad right now."

Jose could feel the lump in his throat and didn't trust himself to speak to her. He kept finding little things to do so he wouldn't have to talk.

Nat continued, "What will you do now?"

"I'm going to move on, perhaps to Lubbock or even farther away."

Nat was startled. Her face looked worried, and she understood that her life would change a lot if Jose left. "But you can't leave!"

"And why not?"

She stammered for an answer that would be convincing. "You just lost Wild Honey, right? Don't you feel as if your heart will break? That's the way I will feel if you leave here. My world will fall apart."

Jose heard desperation in her voice. "It's nice to know some-one cares so much about me. But your world won't fall apart. You have so much going for you now. You and your mother are friends, and she's very proud of you. Your school progress is excel-lent, and next year you'll be queen in the town fair."

"Stop it!" she ordered with a commanding voice. "All that doesn't mean anything to me if you are not part of it." She blushed, deciding that she might have said too much. A big tear came into her eye, and she wiped it away.

Jose felt deeply for her. Her comparing his loss of Wild Honey to how she would feel if he left really made him begin to feel sad for Nat. Could one person love another as much as he had loved his horse?

Nat walked away. He followed her with his eyes, noticing that she walked with her head down. He thought he could hear her sobbing.

Suddenly, he felt hungry. He ate a hearty supper, and he and Jenny talked about his loss. She could tell that he felt as sad as somebody who had lost a close family member. Jose would have to allow time to grieve for his horse in the same way. He could not tell her his thoughts about leaving. But he knew that the ranch would never be the same for him again.

He stayed on for a few weeks, and the matter was decided for him. One day Dr. Luna announced, "I am selling all of my horses, so I won't have any more need of a ranch hand. Your last day will be in a week from today, and I will pay you all of your wages plus the money you won in the race."

Jose felt guilty about taking it. *If only I hadn't raced Wild Honey, he would still be alive*, he thought.

He knew he should tell Nat that he was leaving. Perhaps she had already heard that Dr. Luna was selling his horses and that Jose would no longer be needed. Since the day she had left sob-bing, she had not been back to the stables. Jose decided to ride to her house, and he found Nat and her mother at home. Dressed in a new outfit, she looked prettier than Jose had ever seen her look. Her hair had grown longer and was styled becomingly. Nat's mother left them alone.

"I'm so glad to see you," Nat said.

"I'm happy to see you again too. You look so beautiful in your new dress and stylish hairdo."

"You have come to tell us that you are going away."

He could not read her feelings by looking at her face, and he saw neither sadness nor disappointment in her eyes because she kept a cheerful attitude.

"When are you going?" she asked. "I'll make some cookies for your trip, but tell me a day before you go."

"Let's go for a walk. It may be the last time I'll have a chance to talk to you."

Nat led the way to a spot a few yards from the house. The words she had just heard sounded sad to her, and she was silent. They found a place where they could sit down, and Jose looked into her face. The usual happy, carefree expression was gone. She kept looking at the ground, not trusting herself to speak lest she break out sobbing.

"Why are you so sad?" Jose finally asked.

"Because you are going away. It's like having a very best friend that you grew up with. If this friend moved far away and you couldn't see them anymore, you'd be sad too."

"Yes, it will be sad, but time will heal any pain it may cause you."

"Tell me something," she said as she looked into his eyes. Nat saw honesty and sincerity there. "Have you ever thought you were in love?"

Jose thought for a moment, wondering if he should tell Nat about the crush he had on his teacher. "Yes, I have. I was young and just a high school freshman, and I was in love with my teacher, but our paths separated and nothing ever came of it. You remind me very much of her."

"Have you seen her since then?"

"Yes, I did, when I was at the fair last year. She let me know that we could only be friends since she had married and had a baby. What I decided after seeing her again was that love was really only a fantasy I had. She had never felt the same about me."

"Well, you say that you may never see me again, right? I will miss you so much and will always wonder what happened to you and if you are all right."

He assured Nat that he cared about her too. "However," he said, "I just cannot get serious about someone who is far away from me. This is important for you to understand. I have nothing to offer you, and I can't even say what kind of career I will have. Who knows? Maybe we will see each other again."

The two sat in silence for a few minutes. They had plenty of time to talk, and even in her sadness Nat relished this time she had with Jose. She spoke to him about how her life had changed because of him and how lucky she was to know him.

"Tell me more about your life," she pleaded.

"I'd rather sit and look at you and tell you how pretty you are. I'll miss you more than you know."

"Forget it!" she cut in. "I want to hear it all."

Once again, Jose told his story. He told her how he had returned home after the flood and had never seen his mother and little sister again. Then he told her about the school he had attended when he lived with Paula and Ramon.

"Paula and Ramon were a couple that I was very blessed to have known. Paula was like another mother to me. She was entirely responsible for my getting a good education."

Continuing, he told Nat about his friend Pancho and Burl the bandit.

"Burl was a cattle rustler who robbed banks, stores, and stole stuff from people. His end came when he was killed for resisting arrest. And I may never get over losing Pancho."

Nat had listened closely to all of this, and when he finished, she commented, "You love horses. That's for sure. Now when are you going to love another human being?"

"The time will come, I guess, and I'm sure I'll know it."

Nat stood up and faced Jose. Putting her arms around his neck, she kissed him soundly on the cheek. "Well, I love you," she said. "Let's go."

Jose was surprised by all of this. He followed her back to the house, and she called her mother, saying, "Jose is going to leave us, so he wants to say good-bye."

For a while the three talked together, but Jose had little to say. His emotions were getting in the way, so he decided to ride back to Dr. Luna's. Before he left the next morning, Nat came by and brought the cookies she had promised him.

He headed to town and began checking for jobs in the employment office. He recalled this verse in the Bible: "And we know that in all things God works for the good of those who love him, and who have been called according to his purpose" (Romans 8:28, NIV).

THE KICKAPOO

Jose was uneasy about leaving Big Spring. His thoughts about Nat kept coming back to him. Like so many things in life, there are choices, and perhaps he could love her. The thought haunted him.

His horse plodded along, and Jose, like the horse, was oblivious to the bright blue sky in which clouds hung like giant cotton balls. They moved slowly on this warm day, so Jose settled in for a long ride. He had no idea how far it was to the next town, nor how long it would take to reach Lubbock. He wasn't in the least bit worried about it since he would spend the night under the stars anyway. Also, he had food and the cookies Nat had baked for him.

When the sun was overhead, he decided to stop for a break. There wasn't a ranch house in sight, and he saw no one traveling along the road. His canteen, full of water, was tied to the saddle. He took a bite out of one of the cookies, and he bit down on something hard—it was a small locket. Inside was a little slip of paper that said, "Please write to me." He smiled at Nat's creativity.

Near the end of the day, he saw a lone rider off in the distance. He was moving fast, perhaps because he was trying to arrive at some place before dark.

Jose began looking for a place to spend the night and suddenly spotted a trail that led to a clump of trees. He noticed a little trickle of water oozing from the ground. After digging out a hollow place alongside the trickle, the hole soon filled up, and

Jose's horse could drink his fill. Jose ate a little bit of his food and then put his bedroll on the ground. After gathering some dry grass and dead branches, he lit a small fire. It comforted him, and the heat helped keep away the chill in the air.

The next day's journey led the traveler to cross several crossroads that were little more than trails. The road Jose was traveling had fresh wagon and buggy tracks. By nightfall he reached a small town called Tahoka, where he stopped at an inn, ate a hot meal, and bought some hay for his horse. Then he asked several people about the area nearby and how far it was to Lubbock. They all told him, "It's several hours from here as the crow flies." Before lying down to sleep, he ate another of Nat's cookies.

On the third day of his journey, Jose spotted many ranches near the road. He had finally reached the outskirts of Lubbock, and he wondered if his future would be on one of the ranches nearby. Lubbock was a dusty town and thrived mostly on the cattle industry. He had heard rumors that oil might be below the ground around here someplace, and he could see the drilling equipment on lots nearby. Because the town was growing, many new buildings were being erected.

Housing was scarce, but Jose found a place to rent a room and board his horse. Then he walked down the street. As he walked, he noticed a group of men studying some maps. Smoke-filled rooms were everywhere, and he could see men gambling inside. Others were drinking and talking loudly. He ambled around the town square and sighted the employment office. After fixing its location in his mind, he returned to his room. He thought about what Pancho had told him long before: "*Ask God and He will direct you; read something from the Bible every day.*" So Jose read for a little while, and then sleep overtook him.

Jose awakened before daylight and went outside. He saw people moving about inside their homes, and he could smell the smoke from fires that they had made in their stoves. After eating some breakfast, he went to the employment office to find out about work in the area. He found a job at a store that sold farm machinery. Much of the equipment came unassembled, and it was his job to put it together. Sometimes he was expected to deliver a piece of equipment out to a ranch or farm. That meant he had to take a plow or some other machinery by wagon. This job was usually not a hard one, and if he ran into a problem, he could always ask another employee. When the weather was cold and nasty, he was able to work inside a big shed. By spring, there were several types of farm equipment ready to be displayed and sold.

Jose met a war veteran there in town who had fought in Germany. Ted was his name, and he had only one arm, having lost the other one in the war. He was six years older than Jose and had left home to fight in "the war to end all wars"—that's what all of the politicians said. The United States had been very reluctant to meddle in the affairs of the European nations. Many people felt that the United States should keep strong militarily but not send soldiers overseas to fight other nations' battles.

Communication was slow during the war, and reliable information was hard to come by. When the Germans used poison gas for the first time, the world was shocked! Many soldiers returned home permanently injured by the gas. Ted was not part of that horrible scenario, but he had seen firsthand how it had affected many other men. Twenty million people had been killed in the war, and that number of dead was beyond the comprehension of the whole world.

June came and the machinery was not selling quickly. Farmers were buying tractors, and that meant they could plant much more cotton, a crop that replaced much of the cattle industry.

One day Jose's boss called him in and told him, "You should look for other work because we've got more machinery than we have buyers. You have been a good worker. I just can't afford to keep you any longer."

Jose went to look for Ted and then told him, "I have just lost my job because the farm machinery wasn't selling."

Ted replied, "I'm sorry about that. I wonder if there is anyone else in town who can help you find another one."

The two strolled around town for a while. At the edge of town, they noticed some people who had tied their horses to trees and were erecting tepees. These people were definitely not typical Texans. Nearby, they saw a Model T Ford pickup. The two watched from a distance.

Ted commented, "I'll bet these people are American Indians who have come to perform their dances and to sell what they have made. This is a yearly event, and it will probably last for a few days."

They sat down nearby, and a man who appeared to be in charge of everything approached them. He wore a big western hat, his skin color was of a dark reddish-brown, and his black hair was straight.

"I need somebody to take care of these horses for a few days," said the man. "Would one of you be interested? Your job would be to see that they have enough to eat and drink and also to watch out for them."

Jose spoke up. "I'm out of work, and I'll be glad to take care of them for you. When do I start?"

"Come tomorrow," the man answered. "What's your name? I'm Bluebird."

"I'm Jose, and I'll see you tomorrow."

Bluebird left and the two friends talked for a little longer. They watched the women preparing food over charcoal fires. Then they started walking back toward town. They discovered that they had many things in common and that neither of them had close relatives. Hearing Ted talk about his experiences in the war made Jose begin to wonder if his own father had been in that war and survived it.

Ted never asked for help with anything, but Jose saw where he could lend a hand—like helping Ted button his shirt or tie his shoes. The two spent hours talking about both serious and frivolous things.

Ted told Jose, "I started a delivery service with a horse-drawn wagon. I pick up merchandise at the train depot and deliver it to stores or private homes. Since I have only one arm, some of the larger items give me trouble. If you will, I would like for you to join me in a partnership, and we could add a buggy to offer the public a taxi service."

Jose replied, "I'll think about your offer and let you know soon."

The next day, Jose arrived while the Indians were eating breakfast, and they invited him to join them. He listened to them chatter in their own language, but he didn't understand them. Jose decided that he could speak to Bluebird if he needed to speak to any of the other Indians, since Bluebird spoke English and would be able to translate for Jose.

He told Jose where the horses would be kept and where there was water for them nearby. Except for Bluebird's personal horse, the horses were all typical Indian ponies.

Bluebird said, "I drive the pickup, but I enjoy having a horse with me."

Jose learned more about the Indians from Bluebird. This particular tribe lived in Mexico, and each year they would visit a few cities in Texas, sell their wares, and then return to Mexico. Jose also found out that the Indians and the Americans had once been enemies and that many monuments now mark historical battle sites where men from both sides had died. However, the animosity between the Americans and Indians had ceased long ago.

Bluebird's party consisted of four or five men, a few older women, and a girl. They performed their dances to volunteer crowds and displayed their crafts that had been made during the winter months. The women made moccasins and other things using exquisite beadwork. Various colors and patterns showed the brilliance of the women's artistry. They also sold ethnic foods at the dances. Indian flatbread was always a hit with everyone. In Lubbock, their yearly visit provided some of the entertainment for the townspeople.

Bluebird noticed how much better the horses all looked after several days because Jose would take them to graze where there was abundant grass. Then he brushed them down and gave baths to some as needed. Around noon each day, the Indian women would send out a meal for him. Usually it consisted of a delicious soup and corn tortillas or flatbread.

One day a young girl came out carrying Jose's dinner on her head. "This is for you," she said, setting the meal on the ground before him. "I have to look for dried branches for firewood now."

She got a bundle of sticks together and then returned. "I need the jar back," she said.

The two had never spoken together before, although Jose had seen her working at the camp with the women. Now he wanted to know her name and more about her. She was exceptionally beautiful, he thought, with her long black hair, dark eyes, olive complexion, and trim figure.

Jose looked at her and said, "Thank you for bringing my dinner. My name is Jose. What's yours? Is Bluebird your father? And did you make the dinner?"

The girl looked surprised and a little embarrassed, but she lifted her head proudly and answered him politely. "I'm an orphan. Bluebird is my uncle, and he raised me. I can cook and make a dinner just like the one you just ate. I'm glad you enjoyed it. Bluebird says you are good with horses. Do you like the Indian dances?"

"Yes, I do, and especially when you recite folklore and dance 'The Coming of the White Man.' I don't understand it all, but it's very pretty. You haven't told me your name."

"My name's Star. You will hear the Kickapoo word *hotoke*, which means "star," and that is what I am called. Well, I have to be going now." She left abruptly.

From that time on, Jose tried to catch a glimpse of Star when he was at camp. He had little chance to speak with her, but he didn't feel right about asking anyone about her. He just hoped he would be seeing her more and would then have time to talk to her.

Bluebird was a born talker, and he answered all of Jose's questions. "We came from Muzquiz, Coahuila, Mexico. Our town is right on the Santa Maria River and is made up of several houses built in the typical Kickapoo style. On the surrounding hillsides nearby, each family plants corn on the family lands that have been passed down, according to the Kickapoo custom. Every family has a summerhouse and a winter house. The winter houses keep everybody very warm and are built better than the summerhouses.

The Kickapoo crossed the border at Eagle Pass, Texas. They had done so for many years, and the US government asked for no passport or other legal papers. The Mexican government encouraged them to look for work in the United States; hence, many Indian men made the trip into Texas, Kansas, and Oklahoma. When the migrant work was done, they returned to Mexico until the following year. The Kickapoo have been called the "Keepers of Tradition." They have a long history of defending their lands against encroachment or outright stealing. Their travels as migrant workers have never ended. Some ranchers depend on them every year and even know the day they will arrive. Their camps serve as stopping havens for those traveling through to other points. A few of the Kickapoo permanently established their own homes in Oklahoma and Kansas, but they never forgot their old traditions and language.

Jose and Ted went together to the Indian dances and watched the Indians sway, chant, and move in rhythm to the beating of a single, indispensable drum. Sometimes a bamboo flute would accompany the dancers. Its doleful sound set a somber mood for the story that the dance was meant to tell.

Bluebird announced, "We are pleased to have some Caddo Indians join us in our dancing tonight. Star will be telling some of our Indian stories."

After one of the longer, tedious dances, Star got up and began to speak. She was dressed in beaded deerskin. The artwork and combination of colors showed unusual creativity and excellent craftsmanship. Jose's eyes were riveted on her, and he thought, *Surely there is not another girl in the whole world who is more beautiful than Star. Everything about her seems to be perfect.*

Star began her story in a loud, clear voice. "I'm going to tell you about a coyote, a bear, and a skunk. One day a skunk was on a road, and a coyote came along and said, 'Get out of my way. This is my road.' The skunk didn't move. Then a bear came along and saw the skunk. 'Get out of the way. This is my road.' The bear growled at the little black and white animal. Taking his time, the skunk turned around. He lifted his tail and *whoosh*—you should have seen the bear run! I think he is still running."

The crowd laughed and clapped, and Star began again.

"Now I'll tell you why bats come out only at night. Once upon a time, there was a meeting of all the animals. The bat was there too, but the other animals pushed him away and said, 'You are not an animal; you are a bird. You have wings and fly.' The bat then told himself that he would go to the meeting of the birds. When he arrived, the birds said, 'You are an animal that looks like a mouse. Go to the meeting of the animals.' Poor bat. He didn't know where he belonged. That's why he is embarrassed and does not want to be seen in the daytime. That's all there is to this story."

The crowd clapped again, and Star sat down. This tradition of oral storytelling was started by the Indians. It was one of the few types of entertainment they enjoyed since TVs, computers, movies, etc., did not exist back then.

Jose noticed two boys sitting in the crowd. He hadn't seen them before, and he didn't like their looks. The way they joked and made crude remarks about the performers made him uneasy. He and Ted bought some of the food and went home.

The crowds at the dances grew smaller, and Jose sensed that the group would soon be leaving and moving on to a different town. He felt badly because more than anything else, he wanted to get to know Star better. At first she had seemed to him to be a young girl, but each time he saw her, she looked and acted like a young woman.

One day while Jose was out caring for the horses, he noticed two horses he had not seen before. They were grazing close to a stream of water where Jose usually took his horses.

Jose was about to tie his horse to a nearby tree when he heard a loud scream. It sounded like a wounded cougar. He jumped on his horse and made it gallop to the stream. In less time than it takes to tell it, he took everything in. What he saw shocked him! The two boys whom he had seen at the program were struggling with Star. She was on the ground, and they had put a rag in her mouth. Her dress was badly torn, and both her arms were pinned down. She had scratched the bigger boy's face, and he was cursing her.

Anger such as Jose had never known before banished all caution. Jumping off his horse, he shouted, "Stop it, you brutes!"

He grabbed the hair of the bigger boy and jerked him off Star. The other boy then backed away. Star got up, pulled the rag from her mouth, and covered herself with her torn dress. The boy— bigger than Jose—clenched his fists and was ready to fight. Hate emanated from his eyes.

Jose spoke to Star, "Get on my horse and go home."

She bent over to retrieve something off the ground. At the same time, she filled her other hand with dirt and sand. When she straightened up, she flung it in the face of her attacker. He immediately cursed. Beginning to shed copious tears, he tried to wipe the dirt out of his eyes.

"I'll get you for that!" he shouted to Star.

The two boys went down to the water's edge and tried to wash the dirt out of his eyes. Jose's anger still boiled inside him, but he knew better than to tangle with the two of them. One of them approached him.

"What is she to you? She's just an Indian."

The boy's statement lit a fire in Jose. He could have easily started a fistfight. He looked deeply into the boy's eyes. "She's a human being, and you have no right to molest her." Turning aside, Jose walked away quickly with his hands clenched into fists.

Bluebird saw Star ride into camp on Jose's horse and wondered what had happened. She had been crying and couldn't talk.

When Jose showed up later, Bluebird asked him, "What happened out there? Star's dress is ruined, and her hair is a mess. What do you know about it?"

"Let her tell you," Jose replied. "I would rather not say, and I'm too angry to talk about it."

Bluebird looked puzzled and didn't press the matter.

Jose said, "I will be back in the morning." Then he mounted his horse and found his way home.

He slept very little that night. He kept thinking about what might have happened had he not heard Star scream, and he knew he never wanted to hear a scream like that one again. He thought to himself, *How will Star ever get over this?* He continued to turn and toss, longing to be with her. Was there something he could do to support her?

The next day, Bluebird sat down beside him as Jose's breakfast was served. "Well, we're moving out of here," he said, " but I wonder if you would like to go with us to Amarillo. That will be our last place for the dances this summer and should take two weeks or so. When we get there, you will be in charge of the horses again."

Jose's heart skipped a beat. He thought about being able to see Star for a little longer until the group went back home. Bluebird gave Jose the money he had earned for the days he had worked. It wasn't much, but he was glad to get it. He knew what he would do, but he told Bluebird, "I'll talk it over with my partner. We have a delivery and taxi service to take care of in town."

Jose wanted desperately to see Star and talk to her, but she was nowhere to be seen. His work was over, and there was no reason to stay around the rest of the day. Men were dismantling the tepees, and women were washing pots and pans to be placed on the pack animals. In a few hours, the group would be leaving. Jose went back to town to find Ted and talk to him.

"Ted, Bluebird has invited me to go with him and his family to Amarillo for a short stay."

Jose made no mention of Star or how much he thought of her. Nor did he say anything at all about the attack on her.

Ted, sensing Jose's desire to leave, replied, "I guess you do want to go, but surely not just for pay or food."

"I have made friends with the group, and I believe I can help Bluebird out. I like them, and he knows I do a good job with his horses."

He got his clean clothes together and went back to camp. The horses were ready to go, and the pickup was loaded. Where was Star?

Bluebird explained, "Star went back to the stream where she was molested because that stream was where her fear began. She will be putting the memory aside, if possible, and gathering her spirit again. Then we can be on our way."

Jose had a lot to learn about the ways and beliefs of the Indians, and he wondered what Star would do to recover from that horrible fright. Would what had happened cause her to mistrust other men and even himself?

The party riding the horses got started first while Bluebird finished packing. Jose would be riding with him.

He said, "Now I will show you what to do before cranking up the Ford. The adjustments have to be just right for the spark and gas levers. You have to hold the crank just like this so that if the motor backfires, it won't break your wrist."

The black cushions on the seat were well worn and hard. There were no curtains on the doors, and the wind blew freely through the car. They had to go slowly because of the road. It was poorly maintained, and deep ruts showed where other vehicles had plowed through the mud. It didn't matter because they would arrive at any given point ahead of the rest of the group.

Bluebird spoke up. "What about your background and life? What can you tell me about your family?"

Jose told Bluebird his story and then added, "Besides the death of my mom and little sister, I have also known many friends who died. Once, I had a horse named Wild Honey, and he was really a gem of a horse. I actually raced him twice, although he was not expected to win either of the races. He won both of them, though, and shortly after that I found him dead on the ground. He had been killed in a horrible manner by two men who decided to get back at him for winning the races."

Upon telling this to Bluebird, Jose's voice broke, and big tears streamed down his cheeks.

The two shared other stories, and finally Bluebird told Jose what Star had said about the incident at the river. She told Bluebird that Jose had defended her from the two ruffians and that she was embarrassed to face him again.

Jose ventured a question that had come to him over and over again. "What did she do when she went back alone?"

"I imagine that she bound together a few sticks from the river and then swept the ground of all grass, sticks, and pieces of wood.

She threw them into the flowing water as she chanted. 'Be gone, be gone.' Then she went back to the swept spot and asked the Great Spirit to be with her."

Jose remained silent, thinking about things Pancho had told him long before and also what Kayla's dad had told him about the living God. Jose did not doubt God's love for him, nor the fact that God was interested in every detail of his life.

At last they arrived at a place where Bluebird had stayed once before, and he stopped the car. "We'll stop here for the night. The others will arrive soon, and we'll set up one tepee. The women can sleep in it, and the men can sleep outdoors."

Bluebird showed Jose how to put up the tepee and how to put on the covering of deer hides. Then they dug a hole where a fire could be made for cooking. It wasn't long before the rest of the party arrived. Jose helped with the horses and got them tethered where there was grass. He got only a short glimpse at Star. Perhaps it was just his imagination, but it seemed like she knew where he was. Perhaps her embarrassment prevented her from talking to him.

The party traveled twenty to thirty miles a day, and Bluebird told Jose more about Star. Her mother had given her away because the man she wanted to marry didn't want a baby. Bluebird was a distant relative of the woman, and he had compassion for Star and took her to raise as his own. She always called him uncle, and he had carefully protected her.

Bluebird said, "You know, Jose, those two young bucks in Lubbock had been watching Star and eyeing her as a potential wife. She did not welcome their attention, however, and that was what brought on the attack. She's getting past the age when most girls begin their married lives. She went to school in Mexico and can read and write. Most Indian girls do not go to school. Anyway, her birthday will be coming up soon—before we leave Amarillo."

The dances and sales of beaded goods went much the same as they had in Lubbock. On the second night, during the chanting and singing, Jose looked out over the crowd. Suddenly, he froze inside. There stood the two ruffians who had attacked Star. He knew they had followed the group and hoped to finish what they had started. No doubt the rancor and hatred had built up since Star had thrown sand in the boy's eyes. Jose wondered when and where they would try to get even or when they would get him for breaking up their plan. He looked around for Bluebird because he needed to tell him about this as soon as possible. Star was supposed to dance, but he was sure nothing would happen here with so many people watching. In any case, he would have to be on his guard.

The two boys sat down as though they were spectators. Jose showed Bluebird where they were. He walked right up to them, and without a greeting he looked into their eyes.

"You fellows followed us from Lubbock," he said with a calm, authoritative voice. "You attacked my niece with your evil intent. I'm warning you now to leave here. I don't want to see either of you around. Get out!"

"You don't scare me," the older one said. "This is a free country, and I can do whatever I want to."

Bluebird pulled a knife from a sheath in his belt. He made sure that only the two saw it. His voice was sharp, and people nearby heard what he said. "Leave. Get out of here right now!"

The boys hesitated briefly while Bluebird stood there looking at them. The bystanders, all listening intently, watched as the boys got up hurriedly and left.

LOVE

Two days later, Jose was out taking care of the horses when the two boys caught him by surprise. They had been hiding, just waiting for him. The attack came suddenly. One hit him in the face as hard as he could. Jose's eye began to swell. He received more blows to his body and head. Being outnumbered by the two, his efforts to defend himself against the blows were of little effect. They pummeled him unmercifully all over his body, and he fell to the ground, struggling for breath.

The boys kicked him in the side and left him as they laughed tauntingly. Jose lay there, racked with pain. It took some time before he could even breathe freely. He didn't even have the strength to get up. He did try, but the pain was much worse. Somehow, he finally got up and hobbled back toward camp.

He didn't want anyone to see him, so he looked for a place to lie down. The afternoon sun slowly set into a short twilight, and the Indians sat down to eat their supper. Star noticed that Jose was not there, and she mentioned this to Bluebird. Soon the whole camp knew about Jose's absence. Bluebird mounted his horse and rode around the area, but he could find nothing.

Jose was sleeping and unaware of the search being made for him. During the night he got up and, with painful steps, stumbled into the camp. Bluebird heard him moaning as morning came, and the rest of the camp began to stir. He noticed that Jose's one eye was partially open and the other one was swollen shut.

"Don't talk if you don't want to," Bluebird whispered softly, "but I bet I can guess. Those two boys caught you and beat you up."

Star soon found out about Jose, and she hurried to see him. When she got close and saw his swollen black eye and the bruises on his face, she could not believe it. However, she knew there could be only one explanation. Looking at him tenderly, she spoke so he could hear her clearly.

"You got beat up for me, and right now you are hurting. You took the blows that I might have taken. Those cowards were also mad at Bluebird, so you must have gotten what they wanted to do to him." Star paused and touched his face. "Ever since the other day, I have wanted to thank you for saving me."

Jose drew in a sharp breath, but it caused him to grimace with pain. She could see that he wanted to say something. Putting her finger to her lips, she indicated that he didn't need to say anything.

Jose took a quick, short breath. "Ja-ja-ja-just seeing you makes me feel better," he stammered.

She smiled in a way he had never seen before, and that made him feel even better. Star left and soon brought him a plate of food for breakfast.

Bluebird was watching and asked her, "Can't you see his lips are so swollen that he won't be able to eat?"

Her face flushed red with embarrassment. "He looks like a street brawler who had too much to drink."

She noticed the fresh blood on his shirt. Bluebird saw Star's startled expression and also observed the blood. He helped Jose take the shirt off, and he could see the nasty gash in Jose's side. Jose had not been aware of the wound and could not tell them when it had happened. Star rushed to get a basin of water and soap to clean the wound. When that was done, Bluebird put some salve on it and bandaged it. Jose lay down again and felt better. Bluebird and a helper moved Jose into a tent where the frigid air would not strike him.

The swelling in his face was lessening. The hole in his side began its slow healing process, and Jose was able to talk with some effort. If he coughed or took a deep breath, however, he experienced a sharp pain. Riding in a saddle was out of the question.

As he got better, he saw less and less of Star. Not that he wanted it that way; it was her choice. He wondered if he should go back to Lubbock.

One day, while he was walking around, he saw Star sitting on the ground under a shade tree beading some moccasins. She looked more beautiful than ever with her long, black hair in two braids hanging down her back. She had woven a bright ribbon into the braids and wore a headband of bright yellow beads that had a figure of the Indian thunderbird in the center. It was done in a variety of colors: deep crimson, buffalo red, brown, and cream. The Mayan blue in the breast area was spectacular. Jose admired it for a moment, and then he looked at the beading that she was doing. Although she gave no indication that she knew he was there, she could feel his presence. Their eyes met for a brief second, and Star looked away.

"Are you feeling better?" she asked. "You were beaten up beyond recognition the other day."

Jose chuckled and nervously changed the subject. "Something tells me we are about to move out of here. Is that true?"

"We go when Bluebird decides. How do you feel about it?"

"I have mixed feelings because I need to get back to Lubbock."

"And why is that? Is there somebody special you want to see there?"

"No," he answered honestly. "I have a business to manage—a taxi service with a horse and buggy."

"Maybe you don't like the food we feed you here."

"No, that's not it at all. The food has tasted very good! It beats what I can make. If you tasted my cooking, you would say that even a dog couldn't eat it!"

Now it was Star's turn to chuckle as she remembered some of the men in former days who had tried to cook for the tribe. They had wanted to make things the Indian way but were not at all successful. She looked at those who were busy in the camp. Although she was in full view, she knew that she and Jose shouldn't talk together for very long.

"You better go now," she told him without explanation.

Jose left, feeling sad that he would not be seeing Star much longer. He thought to himself, *Perhaps she does not care for me anyway.* He wanted to leave and bury his feelings about her by staying busy. That way there would be little time to think about such a lovely girl.

The horses were in good shape, but Jose told Bluebird that his horse needed more exercise.

When everyone was ready to leave, Bluebird said to Jose, "You ride my horse for at least part of the day."

Jose replied, "Okay, I'll be glad to." He thought that he might be able to talk to Star as they rode along.

After they got started, leaving Bluebird to follow with the car, Star rode near Jose.

"Bluebird thinks a lot of you to let you ride his horse. There are not many people he would allow to ride him. I thought you probably would not be able to ride yet. Don't you have any pain in your side?"

"It's not bad except when I try to mount," replied Jose. "I'm riding to give this horse some exercise. But there's another reason. I want to talk to you. Soon you will be going back to Mexico and I may never see you again. That makes me sad. I want to hear from you—what you are doing, how it is in your town, and if you will make another trip here next year."

They came to a narrow place in the road. Two horses could barely pass through at the same time. Their two horses pressed together, and for just a brief moment, Jose and Star were very close. She took the occasion to slip him a small leather object. It had solid beadwork all over it. He did not look closely at it right then. He thought she might not want anyone else to know about it, so he put it in his pocket.

That night, Bluebird took Jose aside and advised him, "You better not ride together with Star. That's not the Kickapoo way. Men always walk or ride ahead of the women. The people are beginning to talk about this, and I know you don't want Star to be in trouble."

Now Jose began to feel like he might be in love with Star, even though the two had not discussed it. Jose knew his time with the group was short and that he would have to get information soon if he wanted it.

"Let me ask you," he said to Bluebird as he looked carefully into his face. "Can I visit you in Mexico?"

"And why would you want to do that?" Bluebird asked.

"Because I want to see Star."

Bluebird's expression was unreadable. His sober face showed no emotion whatsoever. After a while, he responded, "Have you told Star, and what did she say? Is this serious?"

"Yes," Jose answered with conviction. "What is the Kickapoo way of telling a woman you love her and that you want to marry her?"

Bluebird let his thoughts roll over in his mind. He had kept Star from marrying at age thirteen like most girls did. He wanted her to have a better life than just raising some children and working hard to feed them. He wondered how the people would receive the information from Jose if he suddenly appeared and started talking about marrying Star. He also wondered whether Star would want to leave her culture and live a new kind of life elsewhere.

"I could tell them you are half Cheyenne or Arapaho. I won't tell them that you are Mexican American because then the young bucks would object strongly."

Jose didn't like this type of deception. This whole thing with Star was probably just a dream anyway. He was encouraged a little bit because Bluebird didn't oppose his seeing Star.

That night, Jose wrote her a note and put it in his pocket:

Dear Star:

I do not know if I will have a chance to talk to you again, so I'm writing this note to tell you how much I love you. If the chance comes, I will tell you personally and not give this to you. I want you to know how I feel. I talked to Bluebird about visiting you in Mexico, and I want to know what you think of it. I'll need to find out how to get there.

Love, Jose

After folding the paper and putting it in his shirt pocket, Jose decided to go to sleep.

The next morning, the party was delayed because a horse had drifted away. They found a broken halter, and the rope was still tied to the stake. Jose repaired the broken strap with a few simple tools. The horse was found, and people made ready to leave. In another day, they would be near Lubbock.

Bluebird was having trouble with his car and knew that he would have to go into town to get some work done on it. He told the party to go ahead and set up camp. This was the same camping spot that they had left weeks earlier. Star made a visit to the large flat rock, and Jose met her as she returned.

"I have come to say good-bye," he told her. "But I must tell you something else. I love you, even though I have nothing to offer you in the way of riches or anything else money can buy. I love you more than anything else in the world and would like for you to be my wife. Together, we can make a wonderful life for ourselves." He reached out for her hands and looked into her eyes for an answer. His heart beat loudly.

She drew backward a step. Without betraying her own feelings for him, she gently replied, "I am not ready to marry. Are you? Perhaps someday—The Great Spirit will tell me when it is time. If it is supposed to be, it will be. We can see each other next summer when we return. By then, you will know for sure if you really want to marry me. I'm just an Indian."

"Don't say that! I get angry thinking about it. You are just as important and as good as anyone else in the world. Besides, I love you for who you are. That's so long from now—a whole year. Promise me you will come back and that you will keep yourself for me."

She could hear the desperation in his voice, but she was unable to make either promise with certainty, so she didn't answer him.

"Can you give me an address where I can write to you?"

"Letters may be few and far between," Star replied. "Some get lost, and others are opened, read, and thrown away. And it sometimes takes weeks to get to rural towns. I don't mean to discourage you. I am telling you this so you will know."

Star and Jose parted, and he went on his way. He felt both happy and sad. Star had not said that she wouldn't marry him. He caught up with Ted as he was delivering some goods in town. Then he went to his room and slept fitfully.

The next morning, he awoke early. It was still dark, and it seemed strange that he was no longer in a Kickapoo camp. Jose remembered the day before, and he supposed the Indians would be up early to start their journey back to Mexico. He really wanted to see Bluebird one last time. As he lay there thinking, his thoughts centered on the wisdom of Solomon, a king of ancient Israel: "Trust in the Lord with all your heart and lean not on your own understanding; in all your ways acknowledge him, and he will make your paths straight" (Proverbs 3:5-6, NIV).

Jose got up and rode out to the camp. Bluebird was packing the car, and the horses were ready to go. Jose got off his horse and approached Bluebird.

"I want to say good-bye to you," he began. "Have a safe trip to Mexico and a good year to come."

Bluebird finished what he was doing and faced Jose. "How about Star? Aren't you going to say good-bye to her?"

"I've done that already," Jose replied. "Are you coming back next year?"

"That's too far off to tell," Bluebird replied as he observed Jose's face. "It's so hard to get a dance group together to go around like we do. There's not much money in it, and some of the men are talking about working on the ranches instead."

Bluebird stretched out his arm for a handshake—white man's way—instead of parting like the Indians would by simply walking away. Jose was sad as he said good-bye to a dear friend. Bluebird had one final word for him: "Don't play with Star's emotions. She is very delicate and feels deeply when hurt. She is also very capable and kind. Whoever takes her for a wife will be getting a fine woman."

Jose mounted his horse and turned toward town. He was deep in thought, and it wouldn't have taken much for him to turn around and accompany the party for a few hours.

One Sunday morning at church, the pastor announced that in the evening service Ted would be telling about his experiences in the war. Jose had not heard much about Ted's past life, so he made it a point to attend the service. Ted began his speech by expressing great appreciation for what the church meant to him.

"I'm not much of a public speaker," he confessed. "But I will tell you my story. I was raised by an uncle in Oklahoma because my parents died when I was very young. There didn't seem to be much of a future for me in Oklahoma, and when the United States got involved in the war, I decided it was my duty to volunteer to serve. There were thousands of men on the boat crossing the Atlantic. Everyone was frightened because of the German submarines prowling beneath the water. They sank many of our ships, and thousands lost their lives. I'm sure you all remember reading about the Lusitania, the British passenger ship that was sunk by the German submarine in 1915. Over a thousand people drowned in fifteen minutes.

"When we arrived in France, we were sent straight to the front lines. I saw the terrible destruction of cities, homes, and lands. Military equipment, ruined by shells or bombs, stood as silent echoes of the enemy's power to destroy. Wounded men were trying to move away from the front. Their blood-soaked bandages and shell-shocked faces were grim reminders of what lay ahead for our men. Some men assumed that they would never come back, and they made special efforts to drink and carouse right before each battle. I was assigned to a medic unit to help those who were wounded and to give them first aid. After I attended them, I would put them on trucks to be taken to a field hospital.

"Some of the soldiers couldn't bring themselves to shoot another man. They died before they could even fire a shot." Ted's voice was choked with emotion, but he continued. "In my case, a bullet shattered the bone above my elbow, and there was no way to save my arm. A buddy tied it tightly to stop the bleeding, and I went to the nearest field doctor, who told me that he would have to amputate. He sent me to the hospital to recover. At the time, I didn't think much about it. But as time went on and my shoulder healed, I became very angry. I thought that God neither loved me, nor did he take care of me. I grew increasingly depressed. The army did what they could, but they couldn't use a one-armed soldier. I returned to the United States with hundreds of men who had been wounded, and some had even been gassed. Others were never able to heal from the mental anguish the war had caused them.

"I returned to my hometown for a few weeks and began to look for a job. At night, I had nightmares about the war. I would awaken screaming with fear because my dreams were so real. Every night I went through the war again and again and again. I visited veterans' hospitals and saw others who had lost limbs. When they saw me and my empty sleeve, they would say, 'You are so lucky to have lost only one arm. Some of us have lost several limbs.' I saw some men in wheelchairs, and some had to use crutches because they had neither a foot nor a leg. Some of these men would never be able to walk, run, have a job, or get married. I began realizing how fortunate I really am. Best of all, I know Jesus Christ is my friend. I have one hand and five fingers, and I want to serve Him with all that I have."

Ted stopped, and the people stood up to honor him and to show their appreciation. Tears were trickling down the faces of some of those in the audience. When the applause stopped, the pastor gave a prayer of thanks for God's goodness. He prayed for the many people who were still suffering from the trauma of the war. Jose felt much closer to Ted.

Ted took God and His Word seriously, believing the truth that he read. His business prospered, and he was able to buy a modern delivery wagon with rubber tires. He also got a better horse.

Jose was not sure what type of work he would do now. He supposed he could work with Ted. In previous times when he had felt unsettled, Jose would plan his next carving project. He had not carved anything in quite some time now, so he decided to look for a good piece of wood with which to begin a new carving. He began carving an Indian in full regalia. He remembered how Bluebird had looked, and the lines in the face of Jose's Indian were clear, well defined, and spoke of power and pride. He did not know what he would do with the finished figure. It took him a week to do it, and much of that time he had been thinking about Star.

Ted invited Jose to go to church with him.

"I'm Catholic," Jose told him.

"Then why don't you go to the Catholic church?" Ted asked. "But that doesn't mean you can't go with me. People will welcome you there."

Jose didn't reply to Ted.

He remembered Pancho's words about praying. He hadn't said that you had to go to a church to pray, but in church there would be people who would pray with and for you. Jose could hear the church bell ringing in the Catholic church, so he decided to go there.

The mass was new to him, and he did what others were doing—taking clues from them as to when to stand up or sit down. After church, the young priest asked Jose if he was new in town and invited him to lunch. After the priest had asked him about his work, his past life, and his faith, Jose spoke up again.

"I may need a job."

"I'll pray to Mary, the mother of God, that you'll find some work you like," responded the priest.

"Mary, the mother of God?" Jose repeated softly.

"Yes. Good Catholics invoke her name for favors they want," the priest assured him. "She intercedes for us before God."

Lunch ended and Jose went on his way, thinking about what he had heard. Later, he told Ted about the meeting and what the priest had said. Ted listened carefully but said little. Then he again invited Jose to attend his church.

Ted and Jose continued their busy business. They also began delivering ice to homes and stores around town.

Jose really wanted to see Paula again to tell her all about what he was doing and to find out how she was doing. One day he sent her a telegram and asked her if she would be interested in meeting him in San Antonio. Some days later, he received a telegram back from Paula saying that she would be visiting Corazon during the Easter season and perhaps he could join them. Jose was overjoyed to hear this and could hardly wait until Easter for his trip to San Antonio.

Because he and Ted worked six days a week, he had little time for himself. However, he visited the library and borrowed books, including some books about the American Indians. Jose wanted to learn as much as possible about the Kickapoos, but he could find little information about them. Some of the accounts of how the Indians were treated by the early pioneers and by the government astonished him, and he became angry. The injustice, broken treaties, massacres, deception, and intrigue gave him a clear picture of how inhumane people could be.

By now Ted had heard much about Jose's early life with Paula and Ramon, so when Jose told him that he had an opportunity to visit Paula and her daughter in San Antonio, Ted said to him, "You go ahead and enjoy yourself. You need a break, and this will be a good time for you to go."

Jose arrived on a beautiful day in April and located Corazon's house in San Antonio. He was excited to see Paula.

"How is Ramon?" Jose said.

"Ramon died two years ago from the flu and pneumonia. I sold all of the cattle and equipment and have rented the land to nearby farmers."

"I'm so sorry to hear about that, Paula, but I'm very glad to see you. Have you seen Vicente, and how is he?"

"I guess he's okay. I haven't heard otherwise."

"And what about the school I attended?"

"Things have changed," said Paula. "We have a new school, and a bus brings in students from the outlying areas. So we also have several more teachers."

After the two of them had talked for a while, Paula asked, "Have you had breakfast yet?"

"No."

Paula prepared a delicious breakfast for him. He was anxious to see Corazon again. She took them around the city and told them stories about the Alamo and other memorial sites nearby.

Time passed rapidly as they talked together. After two days, Jose said to Paula, "It's about time for me to get back home, but

I have really enjoyed myself here with you two. Paula, when I get a place of my own, I want you to come and stay with me for a while."

Paula's face showed real interest in hearing this from Jose, but she said nothing.

When Jose got back home, he continued his visits to the library and wrote a short paragraph about the Kickapoos. He found some information about them in one of the books he checked out. They were from a small town called Nacimiento, a short distance from Muzquiz.

One day, when there was a lull in their work, Jose asked Ted, "Have you ever been in love?"

Ted thought for a while and then he decided not to talk about his life before he had lost his arm. However, he said to Jose, "Who would have a cripple like me?"

Jose, who scarcely noticed anymore that Ted was missing a limb, heard a sad note in his voice. "Forget about your lost limb. You can do anything I can do, and there is no reason why you cannot be in love, marry, and have a family. You just haven't found the right person yet. Really, though, I think I have found my true love, and it is going to continue to be hard until I see her again."

Ted looked surprised and wondered who Jose had met.

"Her name is Star, and I want to see her again as soon as possible. When I was visiting an Indian tribe, I met her and her uncle, Bluebird. She was molested by two big boys, and I saw what had happened and intervened. You see the scar I have here on my trunk? They stabbed me."

"I saw two big boys recently here in Lubbock. Do you suppose they could be the same boys that attacked Star?"

Jose was left a bit shaken by this news. He knew how much he hated those boys. And he planned to get even with them. He spent a lot of time thinking of ways to do it. He also wondered if they would confront him again and hurt him even worse. Jose decided that he might buy a gun. Lots of men carried guns, especially those who worked with cattle on the ranches. They usually came to town with guns strapped to their sides.

"What'll I do?" he asked Ted. "They just might beat me up again."

Ted was quick to answer. "Don't be caught alone in the dark and pray to God for his protection. Believe that He will take care of you—and He will."

Ted's sincerity and his simple answer impressed Jose. He imagined that Pancho would have said about the same thing. Jose remembered having read Psalm 27:1 and Psalm 56:1. When he thought about these, he felt at peace with the world.

Jose asked Ted, "Were you ever scared in the war—like when you were shot?"

"You bet I was," answered Ted. "Everybody was scared. When the shells exploded near me and the bombs dropped, we could all hear men screaming for help. Dead and dying men were everywhere. Who wouldn't be afraid? There were no unbelievers in the foxholes. The vilest of men pleaded for God's help. It's not cowardly to be afraid. It's cowardly to run away."

During the next few weeks, Ted gave Jose some instructions on how to defend himself against an attack. He showed him how to defend against fists and, at the same time, deliver some blows that could weaken one's attacker. Jose was still thinking about the boys who beat him up, and he definitely wanted to get his revenge.

Ted told him, "You must think clearly, and you can't do that if you are angry or want revenge. Do not purposefully injure anyone. I don't like to fight and never did. There are better ways to resolve problems. You must learn about that too."

Jose watched the calendar carefully. Ted listened patiently to Jose's frequent extolling of Star's beauty and virtues.

"How long have you known this girl?" Ted asked.

"Not long," admitted Jose. "But in my heart I know I love her."

"It is so important to know a person well and for a long time before you marry."

Jose looked at maps and measured roads in miles to determine how far it was to Star's village. He wrote to her, but he never mailed the letters because he had no address to use. And he wasn't sure of either Star's or Bluebird's last name.

The beaded ornament Star had given him was on the table in his room. It reminded him of her beauty and talent. He picked it up and noticed something about it that he hadn't seen before. There was a small pocket inside the leather that could barely be seen. He parted the two sides and noticed a small piece of paper. Pulling it out, he read, "Star del Aguilla." That's her name! He almost shouted out loud. He would send a letter to her immediately.

During the next several days, Jose worked hard. The work helped him to forget about Star—at least during the day. He thought constantly about what he was going to write in his next letter to her.

On Saturday, Ted invited Jose to come to church with him.

"And after our morning worship, we will all eat dinner together. You will be very welcome."

Jose had never heard the songs that were sung that morning, but he noticed that most of the people knew the words. They sung as if they really meant it, and the pastor read what Jesus said about forgiveness.

"We all have need of forgiveness. An unforgiving spirit will poison your life and finally destroy you. Keeping thoughts of anger and animosity in your heart will rob you of joy and peace. The lines in your face will be drawn differently. Instead of a bright, sunshiny smile, you will have a scowl and a frown. Remember what Jesus said about repaying evil with good. If someone has offended you or defamed your name, give that person a bunch of roses or a box of candy or a good day's work. He will not soon speak evil of you."

Jose's thoughts centered on the rogue boys and what they had done.

When the dinner of roast beef, mashed potatoes, vegetables, and pie was over, people began to leave. Many invited Jose to come back. But he was barely able to say thank you since his mind was on the letter he planned to write.

As soon as Jose returned home from church, he penned a note to Star:

> Dear Star:
>
> These last weeks have gone by slower than any time in my life. Since I last saw you I have been working, but I think of you constantly. I miss you more than you can know. How have you been? Did you get back home okay? I don't know if you will get this letter, but I'll be waiting for an answer. You can write to: Jose Chavez, General Delivery, Lubbock, Texas.

The days of winter grew shorter, and everyone began to anticipate the cold weather that would arrive soon. Jose used his horse very little and decided to sell it, along with the buggy. He didn't want to buy hay without getting some work out of the animal. It had served him well, and he felt sad when it was sold. A trip by horseback into Mexico was still in the back of his mind.

His hopes and dreams came true when a letter arrived for him. It was very short. Among other things it said, "I am asking the Great Spirit, Kitzihiat, to keep you well." There was no word about the return of the group from Mexico. Star told Jose that she was well, and he was glad of that.

He showed the letter to Ted and asked, "What about this Great Spirit?"

Ted replied discreetly, "Some American Indians venerate Mother Earth or some spirit they believe inhabits trees, rocks, mountains, or some other object. People in India won't kill an animal, bug, or a bird. They believe that the spirit of a dead person may inhabit that animal, so they don't want to harm it. Man is incurably religious; he always believes in something. For example, the person who doesn't believe in a personal God believes everything came about by natural laws. He believes the world has always been here and that we evolved to what we are over millions of years. Life just happened, some would say. Well, that's just a belief—a set of assumptions—that one chooses to believe. The assumptions cannot be proven. Now as far as the Great Spirit— what's the name? There is a spirit who is God. He's bigger than the whole world—bigger than the universe for that matter. He made it all. He put physical laws in place that govern the planets and stars."

Jose listened to the words Ted said, but his mind was on matters that were of more importance to him. He wrote another letter to Star, thanking her for writing and wishing her well. He ended the letter with three simple words: "I love you."

Ted bought new clothes and shoes, and he would check himself in the mirror before appearing in church. He also took his horse and left on Saturday afternoons. Jose suspected him of being attracted to a girl who sang at church. She was the daughter of a local farmer. After a time, Ted told him that he was going to propose to the girl. If she refused him, that would be that.

"I want you to stand up for me when I marry," Ted told him. "I'm aiming for a summer wedding."

"What if I'm not here? I could be a hundred miles from here with the dancers."

"Bring them with you. You can dance at my wedding."

The two men became closer than ever. Between them was mutual trust and confidence rarely seen among men. Whatever

one said, the other respected it, and they loved each other uncon-
ditionally. Ted remarked that it was like Jonathan and David.
Jose thought of how he and Pancho had also shared a friendship
like that.

Jose gave up on definite plans to ride down to Mexico. He had
no horse of his own, and it would be just a few months before he
expected the dancers to return for their yearly tour. He scouted
around for a horse—one that was young and could fit into a variety of situations.

He went to all the horse sales and saw many fine horses. Prices
were reasonable because so many families were giving up buggies and buying cars. Farmers were leaving their horse-drawn
machinery to rust in the yard. They purchased tractors for their
work. It became harder for him to choose an exceptional horse
from a lot of fine horses.

He spotted the horse that appealed to him as it came pulling a buggy to the sale barn. The owner's daughter sat in the
buggy looking sad. She had insisted that her father take her along
because she wanted to meet the person who bought the one pas-
sion in her life.

"Are you selling this horse?" Jose asked.

"Yes. It's a good horse, but we can't keep it any longer. My
mother is sick, and we need the money to pay the doctor."

Jose checked out the horse and asked if he could ride it. The
man gave him the reins, and the horse stood still until it got the
cue to walk. Jose took it out on the road and urged it to run. It
had an easy stride, and Jose made it run faster. It reminded him of
Wild Honey, and he knew this was the horse he wanted.

The girl, about fifteen years old and whose name was Rose,
patted her horse and looked into Jose's face. With a serious tone
in her voice, she asked, "Will you take good care of Beauty?"

"Of course," Jose assured her. "What is your asking price
for her?"

She looked at her father and let him answer. It was evident he didn't want to see the horse go either. He looked over to where the other horses were standing around, waiting on their owners to sell them.

"I raised this horse myself. It comes from good stock—some racing blood and some quarter horse. If you buy her, would you drive us home in the buggy? It's only two miles down the road. Let's start at forty-five dollars."

He spoke those last words with effort. It was obvious to Jose that he loved Beauty as much as Rose did.

"I'll look around a bit," said Jose as he walked away.

He spotted a beautiful black horse with a star on its forehead. The only other white places were on its lower legs. He looked at it carefully as the owner approached him. Horses were just not selling well. In his mind, Jose could picture Star, with her black hair and olive skin, riding this horse. It would make him proud. They talked about the price, and Jose rode it briefly. It shied away from cars, and its general appearance showed that it needed care. He returned to the first horse he had ridden and closed the deal, giving the man the price he had asked.

The buggy ride went by rapidly. Rose was silent, and Jose was sure she was older than she looked. She seemed a lot more mature than a fifteen-year-old. He knew it must be hard to think about parting with her beautiful horse. He asked Rose about her mother.

"What is wrong with her?"

"She needs hospital care."

"How can you visit her without a horse to pull the buggy?" queried Jose.

"We'll just have to walk."

As they drew near the house, Jose noticed a thin, frail woman sitting on the porch. She arose with difficulty as they came near. Her face was pale. As she struggled to breathe, Jose's heart went out to her and to her family. He quickly decided that he would give Beauty back to Rose and her father.

Rose looked puzzled and unbelieving. Her father had gone to the house, but in a minute he shouted to her, "Unhitch the buggy and let Jose take the horse."

Rose could scarcely collect her thoughts because what Jose had just said left her without words. Finally, she managed to say, "Why are you doing this?"

"Because your mother needs help and I want to help her."

"I'll get your money for you," she said with a bit of chiding in her voice.

"You don't understand," he said softly. "You love Beauty, and I can get another horse. I heard somewhere that it is more blessed to give than to receive. Now I must leave."

Taking her hand in his, he said good-bye and walked back to town. He couldn't believe how happy that good deed had made him feel.

Ted and Jose stayed busy with deliveries. Ted's mind was on his upcoming marriage, and Jose was anxiously awaiting another letter from Star. He counted the days when she should be back in the United States, and he wrote several letters to her but he didn't mail them. At night he enjoyed going outside to look at the stars. The vast universe made him feel small. He knew that only a transcendent God could have created this great splendor of lights he saw in the heavens at night. He had studied some astronomy and read about the discoveries that had been made.

As he looked at the sky, all earthly matters faded. He recognized the majesty, wonder, greatness, and mystery of God's handiwork. It was a glimpse of eternity.

ANADARKO

Jose enjoyed the music and being with the friendly people at Ted's church. One Sunday, he arrived late and sat in the back row. He noticed a man and a young woman sitting near the front, but he couldn't tell who they were. During the service, the man stood up and asked if he could speak. That wasn't unusual at Ted's church. When the man started speaking, Jose saw that it was the same man who had sold him the horse named Beauty.

"I want to tell you what God has done for me. I have been careless about attending church and giving my offerings. My wife became very ill, and she was wasting away. The doctor told us she needed treatment, but I had no money. My daughter, Rose, offered to sell her horse, Beauty. She grew up with that horse and loved it dearly. I took the horse to market and sold it for forty-five dollars, and the man who bought it drove us home in the buggy. When he saw where we lived and that my wife was so sick, he simply gave the horse back to us. He knew we needed a way to get to town. What a blessing that was! A total stranger took pity on us and helped us. Today my wife is recovering, and we are here to give thanks to God. This shows how God can work in our lives. He took mercy on me—one who was spiritually sick—and out of sheer grace, he gave me what I didn't deserve or could pay for. I too am well and will be faithful to Him forever."

The people were completely silent, and some had tears in their eyes. Jose sat glued to his seat and listened to every word. He left the church quickly before anyone could delay him since he was a bit embarrassed about meeting these two newcomers.

The next day a letter arrived for Jose, and he tore it open as quickly as possible.

> Jose,
>
> We are well and hope you are too. I miss you, and I have some news you may not like to hear. Bluebird is going to Shawnee, Oklahoma, where he has kinfolk. Also, he plans to go to the big powwow in Anadarko, Oklahoma, where many Indians gather for a week of dancing and music. After that, and if we still have things to sell, we may come by Lubbock as we did last year. That's all.
>
> Star

Jose read the letter three times. He felt crushed, knowing he wouldn't see Star soon. He wondered how he could get to Anadarko and when the powwow would be. He went to the library to try to get information about it, but he had no luck there. It was suggested to him that he might ask some Caddo Indians who lived in Lubbock if they knew anything about the gathering.

Wasting no time, Jose found the address of some Caddos and asked them about the dances. They told him that he would be one of hundreds of visitors who come every year to Anadarko to watch the gala event.

Jose immediately told Ted that he would be going to Oklahoma for the dances in hopes of seeing Star.

Ted said, "You will be at my wedding, won't you?"

He remembered that the wedding was set for June 2 and said, "Of course. This is one event I don't want to miss."

Jose looked at maps to figure out the distance to Anadarko. He would also have to figure out a way to get there. He wrote to Star, saying that he would meet her there, but did not know if she would get it before the group left Mexico.

After Ted's wedding ceremony, Jose felt that he had to stay and mingle with the guests whose faces were familiar to him. One in particular stood out among them all: Rose's. She was talking cheerfully to everyone, and her happiness showed in her pretty face. He hadn't spoken to her since he gave Beauty back to her. The sadness he had seen then was gone. She and her mother came to where Jose stood.

"I want you to meet Jose," Rose told her mother. "Jose is the man who bought Beauty and then gave her back to us. I will never forget his kindness to us."

Jose was surprised that Rose remembered his name, and he extended his hand to the woman. "I'm so glad to meet you and to see you looking well."

She took his hand and gently held it. "I want to thank you for what you did. It helped our family so much." He knew she must have been talking about her husband's return to his faith.

Rose was standing nearby. "You looked great in the wedding party. You must be a good friend of Ted's. He is such a nice person."

"Uh-huh," he responded. "We work together and argue a lot."

"What do you argue about?" Rose asked.

"Just about everything: religion, horses, and who is the prettiest girl around here."

She laughed, and her expression became serious. "I would sure like to hear about that. Come over and we'll go riding in the country. What do you say? Did you ever find a horse you like?"

"That would be fun," he answered eagerly. "I never saw a horse that could compare to Beauty. I can use Ted's horse while he is gone. How 'bout Sunday afternoon?"

"It's a deal."

They parted, and Jose stayed around a bit longer.

Sunday came and Jose rode out to the farm. Rose was dressed for riding, and she welcomed him with a friendly handshake. Her parents greeted him with a wave of their hands.

Rose asked, "Should we take the buggy or ride horseback?"

"We may want to go where the buggy couldn't make it," he ventured.

Rose placed a small bundle behind the saddle, and they rode toward the open country where there were huge fields between houses. Jose observed that the grain was ready to be cut. In fact, there were some fields already cut, and the bundles of grain stood in neat shocks. Soon they would be threshed and the grain would be stored or sold.

"How beautiful! The standing grain is blowing in the wind, and the shocks are ready to be harvested."

Jose couldn't have said it better.

"God has blessed us in giving this land a good harvest," Rose continued.

They rode along while chatting about this and that. The horses walked without a destination in view. Rose pointed to some distant rise in the landscape where there were some hills and rocky peaks.

"Let's go to the rocks," she suggested. "I brought some food for us, and we can eat in the shade of a tree."

Rose's horse turned, and Jose followed.

Motioning northward toward the vast fields, he remarked, "I hope to become part of those who reap the fields. I would like to start here and work, following the harvesters as they move along. I have never done it before, but I can learn."

Soon they arrived at the elevated area. Rose spread a cloth on the ground and put out sandwiches, deviled eggs, pickles, and a homemade cherry pie. She was quiet for a while. Then they discussed Ted's wedding.

"You know, Jose, Ted and his wife share the same faith. That is such an important thing for a man and wife because it allows them to agree on issues that affect both of them."

Jose had never thought about that. He realized she was serious about it, though.

"I could never marry an unbeliever," she declared.

"And who is an unbeliever?" he asked. "I'm Catholic, and I believe in God. Doesn't that make me a believer? What would you say if I told you I had fallen in love with an American Indian girl who believes in the Great Spirit of the earth?"

Rose looked at him quizzically, and she tried to read his expression. She could think of only one thing to say.

"The Bible says that believers should serve as an example to other non-Christian people. It also says that a believer should not marry an unbeliever. What do you mean you're a Catholic? You attend my church."

"My mother was Catholic, and I may have been baptized as a baby, but I don't know that for sure."

"Tell me about your mother," Rose said with real interest.

Jose related the story of the flood and his early schooling and told Rose about the families with whom he had lived. He mentioned his meeting with the priest in town and what he and Jose had discussed.

Commenting, he said, "I really enjoy the people and worship at your church."

Without saying another word to Jose, Rose suddenly picked up her things and was ready to go home. Her demeanor had changed. Was it just his imagination? He wondered.

As they reached the farm, he looked into her eyes and thanked her.

"You want to know who the prettiest girl around is? You are!" he said without a hint of flattery or deception. She blushed and rode away without another word.

Jose found a farmer who hired him to work and help harvest his fields. He gave Jose a team of horses with a wagon on which to load bundles. With a full load, Jose would drive the team to the threshing rig. It was hot work, and sometimes the wind blew the dust and chaff back in his face. After harvesting the wheat on one farm, the owner said that they would be helping a neighbor with his harvest. So it went for a few days until the rig had to move northward where other fields were ready. Farmers there were eagerly awaiting the machine. Jose enjoyed the work, but he couldn't wait until he could go to Oklahoma. He counted the days until the Anadarko dances were to begin. After a week, the harvesting ended and the machine had to be moved.

Finally, it was time for Jose to leave, and he caught rides on buggies, wagons, and old cars until he arrived in Anadarko. The park was being readied for the weekend events. It contained a large platform and some bleachers. Many Indians camped nearby in the woods and fields. Jose heard them talking in several different languages, and some were practicing their dances and songs. He wondered if Bluebird and Star would come. He didn't see the old Ford pickup.

All he could do was wait. He felt helpless knowing he could do nothing to hasten their arrival. Jose read Star's letter over and over, and each time he read it, he felt more uncertain that they would be coming. To get his mind off Star, he took a walk through town and enjoyed looking at all the shops.

After finding a place to stay, he bought some new clothes and a hat. He observed other visitors who were also dressed in their finest clothes. He saw some Indians dressed in elaborate headdresses and beaded clothes.

After buying some food at the booths some of the Indians had set up, Jose ate heartily of the deep-fried bread and succotash. Becoming restless and continuing to wonder if Bluebird and Star would ever arrive, Jose decided to read for a while. He could not concentrate, though. Maybe, he thought, his longing for and anticipation about seeing Star would end like a bad dream.

The night dances were spectacular events. The symbolism of the dances meant more to the Indians than to the white visitors who paid to be entertained. Jose wanted to know more about Indian beliefs and what their customs meant. He saw an old man who had been sitting in the exact same spot the whole time. His hair and beard were white, and the wrinkles in his brown skin were deep and permanent. Jose approached him with a greeting.

"Who are you?" the man asked in a shaky voice. "What tribe do you come from?"

"My name is Jose," he replied. "You don't know me since this is my first time here, but I would like to ask you one or two questions. What do you know about the Great Spirit? Also, how should we treat the earth?"

The old man drew a deep breath and began speaking. "The earth is where we get our food, and we must respect it. If you plow a field, always ask permission before you do it. Respect the sun since it causes the corn to grow and warms us when it is cold. The moon also must be respected because it too is very powerful. We plant the corn whenever the Great Spirit says that it is supposed to be planted. Both the Great Spirit and the ground are like a great chief and his woman. She does nothing without his permission. When you go hunting, ask the Great Spirit to make you successful and lead you to the type of game you are searching for. If you kill a deer or a buffalo, ask forgiveness from the Great Spirit, but he understands that you need meat to live."

Jose listened keenly. The old man's answer led Jose to ask other questions. "What about a man who wants to take a wife?"

"You do nothing without permission. Some tribes, such as the Cheyennes, of which I am a member, say that you may be required to do four tests—four hard things that you have to overcome. If you win, you can be sure your wish will be granted. Be sure you follow Indian customs. Somewhere close to where you live, there is a bluff or a hill with big stones sticking out of the ground. The Great Spirit is there, and you must find out what you need to offer Him. There may be a cave where you can leave tamales or even a live turkey. I can't tell you what it is. I would have to go there and fast for four days. Then perhaps it would be revealed to me what sacrifice you must make."

Both men sat silently with their thoughts. Jose rose and thanked the man for his time, and then he went on his way.

Was he missing something important? he asked himself.

He searched for Star or any of the Kickapoo dancers. Finding none, he felt depressed as he returned to his room. He lay down thinking about Ted, Rose, and her family. He also thought about Pancho's death and Kayla's father. He could almost hear them saying, "*When you are troubled, worried, fearful, or lonely, tell God about it.*" He fell into a troubled sleep.

A noise awakened him before dawn. He lay still, trying to tell what was happening. Somebody was in his room and moving toward the doorway. The door opened and closed again. Jose felt for his new clothing. It was gone, and so was most of the money he had earned while working in the fields. He took stock of what he had; it wasn't much. He became disturbed and angry.

After he had dressed in his old clothes and shoes, his spirits lifted somewhat. Fortunately, he had put part of his money in a shoe, and it was still there. He could buy some new clothes today.

He started thinking about who would want to rob him and why. Stepping out into the road, he began walking and passed a garbage bin and looked in it. There were his pants and shirt! The money was gone, but he retrieved his clothing, and that helped him to feel a little better. Then he returned to his room.

Suddenly, he heard a sound that he realized he had been waiting for: that of a car coughing and struggling to make it up a little hill near town. Hurrying back to the Indian camps, he realized that the dances would soon be over. He saw a man walking in the distance, and he looked familiar. He was moving toward a Model T Ford pickup. Jose felt his heart begin to beat fast. He wanted to yell out to this man who reminded him so much of Bluebird, but he decided that if he were mistaken, he would be embarrassed. He couldn't keep himself from running to the car, though.

"Is that you, Bluebird?" he exclaimed loudly. "And is Star with you?

Upon hearing the anguish in Jose's voice, Bluebird decided to play a little trick on Jose. "Sorry, but she didn't come."

Jose's face showed pure agony. He was speechless, and life seemed to stop. His work in the fields, his coming to the dances, and his planning all seemed to be for nothing. The excitement and fun that he had so looked forward to could not even be considered now. Bluebird turned his face away, knowing that his expression would give him away.

Pointing to a new canvas tent, Bluebird said, "Come with me. I have a tent set up over there."

Jose could not speak, but he stumbled along toward the tent, and Bluebird disappeared inside. Jose stood before the opening, dejected and sad. But then he heard a female voice say, "Come in."

He stepped inside, and it was fairly dark, but his eyes quickly adjusted to the darkness. He saw Star! She stood right there before him, looking even more beautiful than he remembered. He was speechless, and she giggled.

"Aren't you even going to give me a hug or a kiss like the white men do?"

Needing no prompting, Jose took her in his arms and held her tightly. "Will you marry me, Star?"

Hesitating briefly, she answered, "I can't."

All Jose could do was stare at her. But then he noticed that her face was pale and that her body was thinner than before. She coughed, and a deep frown crossed her forehead. Star's facial expression was serious and her words were few.

"I am sick. I have tuberculosis," she told him frankly and deliberately. After a moment, she continued. "I won't give myself in marriage to anyone in the condition I am in. You deserve better. You can go away and leave me and I won't blame you."

Jose was disappointed, and it showed on his face. He was not sure he heard correctly or understood what she had said. His usual active mind was befuddled since it sounded to him as if he might lose Star also. Bluebird entered the tent and guessed what was being talked about between the two. He and Star had seen a doctor in Mexico who urged them to go to the United States for treatment. There, they had confirmed that Star had active tuberculosis, and they also received the standard suggestions for treatment.

Jose looked at Bluebird, expecting him to tell him that this was not true. His heart began to cry out, *Can Star be cured and how?*

Bluebird summed up all that they had learned. "Star has a bad case. She began coughing and spitting up nasty-looking stuff back in Mexico. The doctors there diagnosed tuberculosis. The only known treatment is to have the patient eat well and rest. They also told us that living in a warm, dry climate is best. Star would have to be isolated in a special sanitarium for tuberculosis patients. Here in the United States, the government will pay for her care. It could take months or a year to fight the disease. Some people get well, and others do not."

These grim facts left Jose speechless.

Star, seated on the floor, began crying softly. Her future seemed dark and uncertain. Her usual good health and vigor were gone. She couldn't help but think, *Maybe my best friend will soon be gone also.* Time seemed to stop, but finally Jose spoke.

"What do we need to do? Have you made any plans?"

Her heart leaped for joy when she heard him say the word *we.* Jose was including himself in helping her get well.

"We'll find a way," he said confidently. He sat down and put his arm around her.

Bluebird left and went out to work on his car. Jose and Star sat in silence for a few minutes.

He looked tenderly at Star and said, "We'll get through this together, and you will get well."

Star remained silent—as though she knew more than what she had just revealed.

Jose commented, "I love you dearly, and starting now, we'll look for the best way to make you well. You look great, and it's hard to tell that you have anything wrong with you. I'll be back later, and we'll go see the dances together tonight."

He looked up into the sky, and by the sun's position, Jose guessed that it was around noon. Bluebird looked surprised that Jose was leaving.

"Where are you going?" he asked.

"I'm going to find out about this…what did you say it is that Star has? I have to know what we can do. Come along if you like."

The two walked into town and went to a local doctor's office. They were greeted warmly and asked what they wanted.

"Tell me about tuberculosis," Jose said. "This man's daughter was told she has a bad case, and I want to know how to help make her well again."

They were told to sit down and wait for someone to talk to them. The waiting was hard, and Jose wanted to be with Star.

Bluebird said, "When I talked to the doctors, they asked me if Star got short of breath, if she had a cough, and if she had any blood or rusty streaks in her sputum. He also told me that little bugs are in her lungs."

Soon a doctor appeared, and Jose and Bluebird were taken into a room where they could talk privately. Many pictures hung on the wall that showed parts of the human body, and some showed where tuberculosis is sometimes found. Jose drew encouragement from the doctor's first words.

"How can I help you?"

Jose explained briefly that Bluebird and Star lived in Mexico and were advised to come to the United States to get treatment for Star's tuberculosis. "We are here to find out about the best treatment for her."

"Unfortunately," replied the doctor, "there is no medicine to cure tuberculosis. But people usually survive if they can make changes in how they live. The patient should go to a sanitarium—a hospital-like place—where only people who have tuberculosis live. There, they are given good food, plenty of rest, clean air to breathe, sunshine, and a clean environment."

"And where might the nearest sanitarium be?" Jose asked.

"Well, the closest one I am aware of would be in Albuquerque, New Mexico," the doctor replied.

Jose interrupted with another question that had been burning in his mind. "How long does it take to get well?"

The doctor shook his head. "We can't ever tell. It depends entirely on the person, as well as how advanced the infection is. I would say that it would take at least a year." Pausing, the doctor looked at the two men. Jose and Bluebird were thinking about how this decision would affect not only Star's life but also theirs. "If it were my decision to make, I would look for a pleasant spot about four thousand feet high—one that has trees, lakes, and not too many people. If you will bring the patient to see me, I will examine her. Then I can give you a letter to take to the sanitarium you choose for her."

Jose and Bluebird returned to camp. They bought Indian food for their supper. Star had dressed in her best clothes. To anyone but Bluebird and Jose, she looked healthy.

In a serious manner, she said, "Where did you two go?"

After Bluebird explained all that the doctor had said, Star looked pensive.

Then Jose exclaimed, "You are going to get well!"

The three of them went to the dances and sat in the upper bleachers. The beadwork on Star's dress and moccasins brought about many looks from those sitting around her. She had two eagle feathers in the band around her head. Taking a feather out of the band, Star wove it into the band on Jose's hat. This indicated that there was a special bond between them.

The sun had set and the sky was clear. The giant afterglow gave way to the darkness of the night. A dark cloud of another kind hung over the hearts of the three visitors.

That night, none of them slept well. Jose's optimism faded into thoughts of Star's long stay in a hospital. Bluebird pondered over where she might go to get the best care. Star knew she would have to face the fact that she might not get better at all. She had seen some of her people die of the same disease that she had. She thought of ways she could implore the Great Spirit to help her.

The next morning, they all went to see the doctor. He gave them a letter that they could use when they found a place for Star. Constantly, they pondered the question "Where should we go?" Finally, they decided to head for New Mexico. Bluebird had calculated that it would take five or six days to get there, if all went well. Jose wasn't too pleased, since he wanted Star to start treatment as quickly as possible.

The trip was arduous, and Star had some coughing spells that made Jose more anxious than ever. He thought about what the doctor had said in looking for a place where the summers wouldn't be too hot.

Upon their arrival in Albuquerque, they saw many Spanish and Indian people. After asking directions, they found the sanitarium, and it looked new. The grounds were clean and well kept. Patients who were sitting outside or walking around were dressed in white. Star wondered what it would be like inside.

The next day, she was accepted as a patient. The staff questioned her at length and even took X-rays. An X-ray machine, a fairly new discovery, had not been available to doctors in the smaller towns where Star had been. At last they could confirm her diagnosis. She was given clean clothes and shoes and taken to her room. It appeared spotless and had a single bed and a dresser. She had been given several sheets of paper about the sanitarium and the rules that were to be observed, so Star sat down to read.

There was a waiting room out front where visitors could come to see their friends or family. Nurses and doctors seemed to be hard at work, and signs warned against spitting on the ground. Sneezing and coughing were to be done with a handkerchief over one's face.

Once Star got settled in her room, she went to find Jose and Bluebird.

Jose said, "I am going to look for work near here so I can be close to you. If I can't find work here, though, I will have to go to another town."

In any case, Jose promised Star that he would write her regularly. Bluebird decided he would go to Eagle Pass and visit some Kickapoo relatives there.

Saying good-bye was difficult for all of them. It was like bidding farewell to a soldier brother who was leaving to fight a war in a far-off land. Both Star and Jose shed tears as they embraced.

Jose said, "I'll see you before too long. We are in this together, and I will pray for you every day."

"I hope your God hears and answers your prayers," Star said with feeling. "Come back as soon as you can."

He pulled from his pocket the last twenty dollars that he had and pressed it into her hand. She did not look at it but put it in the pocket of her dress.

Bluebird hugged her and said, "I will try to get back to see you before a year has passed."

Star gave him a pair of moccasins that she had been working on. "Sell these if you need money. I can make some more."

The next day, Bluebird went on his way. Jose walked the dusty streets of Albuquerque in search of work. He stopped by the employment office and completed a form that they required. He was qualified only to work with horses and cattle. Having no local address, he told the people that he would check back the following day.

That night, he found an old cardboard box and used it for a mat to sleep on in an alley. After counting his money, Jose saw that he had a mere ninety cents to last him until he could find a job of some kind.

The next morning, he was awakened by a city policeman who was looking for somebody who had stolen some goods from a store. He ordered Jose to stand up and then searched him for weapons.

Then the policeman asked, "What is your name, and where are you from? Also, where were you yesterday?" Another officer came around the corner.

Jose answered forthrightly, knowing that he had done nothing wrong. "Most of the day I was at the sanitarium," he said. "I have a friend who was accepted there because she has tuberculosis."

"Let's go over there," one of the officers said to the other. "We'll find out if the girl is there and whether anyone remembers seeing him yesterday."

The policemen entered the sanitarium with Jose between them. They questioned the staff and found out that there was a second man with Jose.

Looking suspiciously at Jose, the officers asked, "Where is your buddy?"

"I don't know because he left in his car for Eagle Pass yesterday."

The officers didn't check this information out with Star but said, "Better come along with us until we recover the stolen items or find the thief."

Jose ended up in jail. He was puzzled and discouraged, but he had a bed, and they gave him food.

Noticing some officers riding horses, he called a guard to his cell and asked, "Do you have anyone to groom these horses?"

"No, we don't," replied the guard.

"I'll be glad to groom them if you will let me out of my cell here."

After consulting with the warden, the guard came back and opened the door. Jose was led to a barn nearby. Other horses were there, and all were in need of currying and brushing. He was happy because he was busy and the time passed rapidly. He wondered about how Star was doing.

Soon the guard came and led Jose back to his cell. He offered to work with more horses the next day and the days after that.

Two weeks went by, but no one said a thing about his case. One day the warden came and said, "You can leave now. They found the man who stole the goods from the store."

The two officers thanked Jose for grooming the horses. Then they handed him four dollars.

One of them asked, "Where are you going now?"

"Wherever I can find a job. I may go to Lubbock. I lived there for a while and know some people."

One of the officers spoke up. "I take my kids to ride ponies at a place out in the country. They have lots of horses, and now may be a good time to ask about work there. They even rent horses to go on long trips into the mountains."

Jose got directions to the place. He thanked the officer and hurried away. Then he went to see Star, who was surprised to see him.

"Where have you been?"

"In jail," he answered.

She was shocked, but after Jose finished telling her the details about his misadventure, she laughed, and the sound warmed Jose's heart.

"It was okay, I guess," commented Jose. "I had a bed, food, and they treated me well. Now tell me how you've been doing."

"This is a good place," said Star. "We have lots of rules to observe, but the food is good. I sleep a lot and rest even more. I can read and do some sewing or beading as long as it doesn't tire me out."

Jose told her about his possibility for a job. "I hope this works out for me so I can be close to you. Tell me more about how it is to be here."

"Well, we don't have any doorknobs on the doors," she began. "They say it helps to keep the bad bugs from spreading. We wash our own dishes and dry them out in the sun. They give us clean clothes every other day, and anyone who coughs has to cover his mouth. We spit in a paper, and then they burn it. We are allowed to walk outside or sit in the chairs under the trees. Also, we can do simple exercises but not to the point of getting too tired. We rest a lot. It's part of the treatment."

"Have you seen a doctor?" Jose asked.

"I expect to see one in a day or two," answered Star. "He's a young man, and this is his first year of service since medical school. I've been told his name is Dr. Watkins. That's what I heard anyway. Here is the money you left with me. I don't need it. Take it and look for a place to stay tonight."

Jose left and rented a room. The next morning, he found the place he was looking for and began working that same day. He checked over some of the horses for anything that needed attention. Things really got busy when parents brought their children to go riding.

Jose worked an entire week before he visited Star. He was off on Sunday. In addition to things he needed to do for himself, he wanted to make as much time as he could to be with Star. Arriving at the sanitarium around four o'clock, he found her beading. They were both glad to see each other once again.

Star said, "I had a discussion with the doctor, and he asked me many questions about my background. Then he explained that a recent X-ray showed no significant change in my disease. He also wanted to know if I was eating the foods and drinking all the milk they are giving me. But he asked me questions that I felt were unnecessary and volunteered information about himself that he didn't have to share with me."

"Like what?" inquired Jose.

"Oh, just that he was single and had no girlfriend. Now tell me how your work has been going."

"The boss told me he was glad to see me and that he had a lot of high school kids working during the summer when school was out. But none of them took care of the horses like I do. I am reminded so much of when I worked for Sommers in Big Spring. I told you about that. Perhaps when the weather changes, there won't be so much work. By then, you should be able to go for short rides. There are some interesting places around here to visit."

"The doctor said I should keep up a positive outlook because that would help me get well. I would love to visit those mountains that we see in the distance. To be able to breathe in the fresh air that makes the trees waver and to listen to the air rushing through the branches seems like it would be heaven. I hope the Great Spirit Kitzihiat, who lives in the eternal hills, will help me get well. And I have been looking for signs that he is aware of me. The other day I saw two eagles flying overhead and a feather floated down. It landed in the yard, so I ran to get it so I could bring it into my room."

Jose listened attentively to her every word. Their time together passed too quickly, and finally he had to leave. Star watched him walk down to the entrance and turn around to wave. She waved back and went to her room to take a nap. The young doctor had been watching her, although he was pretending to be doing something else.

The following Sunday, Star noticed some visitors arriving at the sanitarium. They were there to hold a church service. One carried a portable pump organ, and another carried a few books. After they had arranged the chairs in the waiting room, a nurse on duty went up and down the hall to invite the patients to the meeting. Some were too sick to attend, but several others responded. Those who were familiar with the hymns sang loudly, and Star listened.

She noted that the man who prayed spoke as one who was talking to a real person. He asked God to bless and help all those who were sick. An elderly man gave a short message from the Bible. He read of Jesus healing people who were without hope—people who had incurable diseases. He also said that all people had hearts that were sick and needed to be made well. All the bad things one had ever done needed to be forgiven. He showed from the Scriptures that our hearts could be made as white as snow and that we would no longer need to feel guilty before God.

Star wanted to read the Bible for herself, and she asked some of the patients if they knew where she could get one.

"You may use mine," one of them offered. "Take it and I'll ask you for it when I want it back."

That day, Star put aside her beading and read. "In the beginning, God created the heavens and the earth" (Genesis 1:1, NIV).

She stopped and thought about what that meant. God, who created, is above and outside that which He made. He must be all-powerful to have made the universe. She read on and found out that God created the plants, animals, fishes, and man. The book said, "So God created man in his own image" (Genesis 1:27a, NIV).

Star concluded that something about man is godlike. Unlike animals, man can talk; God speaks. Man loves; God loves. Man is able to appreciate beauty and design, and so can God. Man worships a supreme being; animals do not. Man reasons and invents; animals, if they do so at all, do so in a limited way.

Jose came to visit her again that same afternoon. Happiness spread over his entire face, and he appeared jubilant.

He said, "I got paid well, and I will be taking a five-day trip into the high mountains with my boss and his friends from Texas."

They talked together about more trivial matters. Finally, Star showed him the Bible she had been reading.

Jose said, "I still have my New Testament, but I just don't read it very often."

"Do you remember those boys who beat you up?" she asked. "Are you holding a grudge against them, or have you forgiven them for their cruelty to you? I realize it has been some time ago and you may not think of it often, but it still lies there burning and festering in your heart like this disease inside of me. That bitterness and hate has to be cured and the past swept clean."

Jose did not like the direction in which this conversation had gone. Whenever he thought of the time that he was beat up, he felt the same emotions all over again. He could do nothing about it. He hated those boys.

"That's all in the past," he told Star. She talked a little bit about the church service that morning.

Jose asked her, "How is your treatment going?"

"Well," replied Star. "My cough is much better, and I can walk two miles without having a breathing problem. Also, I sold some of my beadwork, so I need to buy more supplies." She did not tell Jose that the young doctor offered to get her what she needed from a supplier downtown.

Jose left after embracing Star in a loving hug.

Some of the patients knew about the relationship between Jose and Star because she had told them. She made a close friendship with a girl who had tuberculosis, but in addition she had a broken leg that had become infected. The girl had ridden a horse most of her life, but one day she jumped off the horse, her leg broke, and the doctors discovered the infection. Her prospects of getting well were good, but she was told never to think of riding again. Her name was Mary, and Star loved her dearly. They talked to each other every day and were not hesitant to share everything that had happened to them. Mary told Star that the young doctor paid a lot of attention to her also when she had first arrived at the sanitarium.

"He seems to think any girl should fall for him. He will hang around until a girl believes he cares for her. Then he loses interest in her. More than one girl has cried over him. Actually, he shouldn't be talking to patients except as it regards their medical condition. He doesn't seem to care about what is appropriate, though."

Star listened and wondered if she had been discreet enough when talking to the doctor. She told Mary, "He offered to get me some things from town."

"And he'll insist on paying for them too," Mary told her with some emotion.

Star laughed at the idea and told Mary that she and Jose were in love. "It sounds to me like the doctor hurt you, Mary, and you are quite bitter about it."

Mary changed the subject and talked about the Thanksgiving and Christmas holidays that would arrive soon.

One day she said to Star, "For many years, my family and I spent Christmases in the high country of Colorado. The snow that covered all of the trees made the world look quite enchanted. The rides in a horse-drawn sleigh in the moonlight were unforgettable."

Star could think of little to tell Mary about her early memories of Christmas. The Kickapoos had little to celebrate. One day was like another.

A patient who had been in the sanitarium for a long time told them how Christmas had been celebrated in previous years. It usually ended with a party where a group from one of the local churches came with goodies to share. They brought cookies, popcorn, fruit, and other things for the patients. This was the only time children were allowed to come into the building. They presented a short program of songs, poems, and dramas. For some of the patients, seeing the children and hearing their laughter and joy was the high point of the whole year.

Mary started having to use a crutch as she walked. She looked worried about this, and her face was sallow. Star knew something was wrong, and her heart went out to her friend.

"What's wrong?" she asked.

Mary confided softly, "They may have to amputate my leg. The infection is destroying more bone."

Star put her arm around Mary. This was enough to let Mary know how much Star cared about her.

After a few minutes, Star ventured, "What do you know and what do the doctors say?"

Mary hesitated before answering. "If I lose my leg, the disease goes with it and I'll be well. If they don't do anything, I may get well but I'll be crippled. Or I could end up in a wheelchair."

Star saw the anguish in her face and yearned to help her. "When will the operation be?" she asked Mary.

"After some of my family can come and give consent," she replied. "I don't want them to see me like this. I came to be cured, and now I'm worse!" A tear rolled down her cheek, and Star wiped it away.

"Don't despair," she said softly. "I have a feeling something will change for the better."

Just then, the young doctor walked by, and he gave a disarming smile to Star. He also observed Mary's crutch.

"What's this?" he asked. "You don't seem to be doing so well."

Mary didn't answer. The lump in her throat was as big as the pain in her leg. The doctor went on his way, and the girls parted.

"I'll talk to you soon," Star told her. "And I'm asking the living God to heal you. Believe that he wants you to be well."

Star went to her room and lay down. Her body was rested, but her mind was not at ease. She reached for the Bible on the table beside her bed and turned to the Gospels where Jesus had performed many miracles. She read about the man whose young son was tormented by a demon. The father had taken him to the disciples, but they could do nothing. When Jesus came by, the man asked him to show mercy and heal his son. Jesus told the man to believe and his son would be well. The father of the boy then asked Jesus to help him believe. Jesus ordered the demon to leave, and the boy became well in an instant. She continued reading about the man whose arm had withered away. It was useless, and Jesus commanded that he stretch it out. When he did that, the arm was completely normal. In this way, Star learned about the promises God makes to people to answer their prayers. She began to pray for Mary.

At the next Sunday service, the leader asked if anyone had a need and would like to have prayer for it. Star told them about Mary and that she might lose a leg. Although they didn't know Mary, several people prayed fervently for her healing.

Star prayed to God for the first time. "Please, God, heal Mary's leg. As you touched the eyes of the blind man, touch Mary and make her well."

When Jose came to visit, Star told him about Mary and about the prayer for her.

He listened and then asked nonchalantly, "Did anyone pray for you?"

THE HEALINGS

The work at the stables was never ending. The horses had to be fed and cared for, and there were repairs to be made on corrals and fences. Saddles and bridles needed attention so that no accidents would occur when customers were riding. In addition to that, Jose had to give some of the horses their exercise. He learned which horse was his favorite to ride and used it on his trips into the mountains. Also, he kept close watch on the hooves of all the horses so that none of them would stumble. His boss, Nelson, told Jose they would be moving a number of horses to a more remote area. There, less work would be required to care for them. So Jose moved two or three horses at a time to the ranch where there was food and water. In the spring, some of the mares would have foals.

The autumn days were getting shorter, and Jose had more time of his own. He borrowed books from the library and read almost every evening. If he liked a particular book, he told Star about it, and she would often read it also. Sometimes he felt sad that he couldn't see her more often. If the feeling was strong and he felt restless, he opened the New Testament and read in it.

One night he began reading in the book of Luke and realized that the story was about Jesus's birth. Soon, it would be Christmas, and he became determined to make an effort to go to the Catholic church in the valley on a more regular basis. Then he started asking himself if he believed—really believed—what he had read. The Catholic service was all in Latin, and it was mysterious. He felt empty inside and wondered where he could find lasting spiritual satisfaction. The peace that people sang about at Christmas had escaped him.

On one of his excursions about town, he saw a small building that had Spanish lettering on it. People inside were singing Spanish-type songs with words about Jesus. The door was open, so he drew closer to listen. The songs were beautiful, and it had been a long time since he had heard such music. He didn't go into the church but decided he would come back soon.

The next Sunday, he was up early and prepared to go back to the little church. When he arrived, he noticed several men, women, and their children who were waiting for the singing to begin, so Jose found a seat and someone offered him a hymnal to use. This book had no notes. A leader announced that they would be singing Christmas songs, most of which were familiar to Jose. He began singing along with the others and one song really touched his heart. It was sung to the tune of *Silent Night*, and it spoke of peace and quietness of spirit.

The talk that morning was given by one of the men who dressed in ordinary work clothes. He spoke about worship. The wise men sought the baby Jesus, and they worshiped him. They recognized that here was a baby different from all others and he was worthy of their adoration and praise. They gave to him gold and other precious gifts.

"We don't know much about those magi," the man said. "But they knew that they had seen the King—one who was destined to rule the whole world some day."

Jose listened carefully to the speaker.

"People don't mind talking about worshiping God the Father, but when you talk of worshiping Jesus, some object very strongly. However, we find that when Jesus was an adult, he never rebuked anyone who worshiped him. Some bowed down on the ground before him. He claimed to be equal with God and said that the Father had sent him here. Man should honor the Son as they also honor the Father. So how can we worship Jesus? We speak to him. We tell him he is worthy of all honor and praise and that he alone is Lord and Master of our lives. We should live our lives by serving him, obeying his Word, and worshiping him. Everything we do, say, or think will show others that Jesus is the center of our lives. As we go about our daily tasks, what we do should reflect that our work is for the King, our Savior and Lord."

Finishing his talk with a challenge, the man said, "You probably won't worship the Lord unless you get to know him. How can you do that? By taking seriously the things he has said in the Bible. Read it and believe."

The words stirred Jose's heart in a way that nothing had done before. There were times when he remembered having talked to Pancho, Ted, or Kayla's father about God and how He claimed people's lives. Pancho had buried those serious thoughts in the business of his work, though he knew deep down inside himself that God was calling him. Jose had always felt self-sufficient and capable, but these people had something he didn't have. He wanted to find out what it was.

Meanwhile, Star was struggling with her problems. She wanted to know if she was improving after months of rest and a good diet. She would ask Dr. Watkins next time she had a chance. She didn't have to wait long because he called her into his office one day. After greeting her pleasantly, he asked her to sit down.

"You know, you are so beautiful. You remind me of stories about ancient Egyptian queens with their dark complexions, perfect faces, and piercing eyes. Or you could be the Grecian goddess portrayed in sculptured stone—a perfect body envied by all women." He paused, and Star wondered where this was leading.

"Look," she said. "I want to know how I am on the inside. Am I getting better?"

Not answering her immediately, the doctor hoped to make their time together last as long as possible. He pulled a bag from under the desk and pushed it toward her.

"I was downtown and picked up some beads, leather, and stuff I think you can use. I really admire your beading and would like to buy something from you."

For a moment, Star was without words. Looking at what he had bought, she put all other thoughts aside. "Well, how much were the beads? I'll get the money for you."

He responded with a disarming voice. "Nothing. I want to give these to you."

This confused Star even more, and now she just wanted to get away from him. In frustration, she asked, "How does the latest X-ray look?"

Taking a long time to look at it, he said, "It looks good. I believe the disease is contained—that is, it is not worse than before—and that is encouraging."

Star stood up to leave. Dr. Watkins didn't look too pleased, but he opened the door for her. "You forgot something."

Her soft voice indicated no displeasure on her part—or so he thought. "I'll get the money for you," she promised.

When she got back a few minutes later, the doctor was gone and so was the package of beads. Star was puzzled and confused. No one had ever treated her like this.

Mary came to see her, and Star told her everything that had happened.

"The doctor likes you," Mary said with conviction. "But then he has liked all the pretty girls who have come in here. He has a big problem. He thinks that any single girl should fall for him, but don't worry. He'll get over it."

Star wasn't so sure about that. She knew there would probably be another encounter. She looked forward to Sunday, when Jose would visit her. She knew he loved her, and although they both had a strong desire for physical intimacy, they willed themselves to restrain from it unless and until they were married.

Mary wanted to attend the church meeting with Star on Sunday. She was overjoyed and full of life as the two of them joined the others. Star was delighted to learn of a positive change in Mary's case. Privately, Mary told her that the doctors had decided to postpone any operation. The X-ray had shown a change, and perhaps a cleaning of the bone would be all she needed.

"God has answered our prayers," Star commented.

When the whole group learned of Mary's improvement, they praised the Lord and kept praying for both the girls. The group sang the Christmas hymns and listened again to texts from the Bible regarding the birth of Christ. Two prophets who wrote hundreds of years before Jesus was born told about a virgin who would bear a son and that it would happen in Bethlehem.

That in itself, Star thought, *is proof enough that God was overseeing the birth and life of Christ.*

Here was a case where the parents knew the baby to be born would be a boy. She thought of the young girl who was espoused to Joseph. Mary, Jesus's mother, must have been terribly embarrassed and ridiculed when she showed signs that she was with child. In spite of the ridicule and accusations that might come, she said, "Let it happen as the Lord has said. I am his servant." This prayer left Star almost breathless. It was so beautiful and pure.

A few words that had been spoken by the angel were fixed in her mind. They were about a Savior who would come to earth as a baby, and his name was to be called Jesus because "he will save the people from their sins" (Matthew 1:21b, NIV).

Star quickly related this truth to a part of the prayer she had repeated many times with the group: "Forgive us our sins…deliver us from evil…" She knew she was in need of God's forgiveness, and she wanted to be clean. It became a burning desire within her to know that her sins were forgiven. Her own sickness became a metaphor for her spiritual state. She realized her soul was sick and that the only way she could be made righteous before God was to trust Christ in his forgiveness of her sins. Also, her faith in God needed to be strong.

The fact that she had trusted and respected the Kickapoo god, Kitzihiat, made her a sinner. She remembered the Bible verse that said, "You shall have no other gods before me" (Deuteronomy 5:10, NIV).

Star renounced the past and asked that God forgive her for all she had ever done. She promised God that she would follow His way.

Immediately after voicing her prayer, she felt a great load lifted from her heart. Peace and joy replaced the doubt and fear that had been there. She thought of the book by John Bunyan that she and Jose had read. In *Pilgrim's Progress*, Pilgrim had carried a heavy load on his back as he traveled about. He came to a hill on which stood a cross. As he reflected on the meaning of that symbol, the burden on his back rolled away.

Mary and Star asked for permission to bake some Christmas cookies that they could share with the other patients. They were told that this was a highly unusual request but, since both of them were almost well, they could do it. However, they must carefully avoid anything that might spread the germs. The two worked hard, making a huge dishpan full of nutritious cookies. They wrapped each one in wax paper and distributed them to those who were in their rooms. Each wrapped cookie carried a wish for a Merry Christmas and recovery from their sickness. Star kept a cookie for Jose and one for herself. They didn't forget the staff and left cookies in each of their offices.

Star was waiting for Jose when he arrived on Sunday afternoon. They went outdoors to sit in the sun. It had snowed overnight, so they had to bundle up in heavy coats to keep warm. Everything looked so clean and beautiful.

"I bought this plant for you," Jose began. "It's so pretty. It reminded me of you. It's pure, lovely, and brings joy to people who see it."

Star took the flower and looked at it carefully. She noted the symmetry and the delicate pollen stems. It was a large red poinsettia.

"Only God could make such a flower," she commented. "Some say it all happened by chance, but that takes a huge leap of faith. Where is the evidence?" She continued her musing. "The grass withers; the flower fades."

Jose looked at her quizzically. "You are quite a philosopher. Tell me how your week went."

She told him about Mary and how the doctor had told her that she was much better. Then Star gave him the cookie she had saved. They talked about Christmas and what each one would want if it were possible to have anything they could.

Star said, "I would like to be with my people in Mexico, but I want you to be there with me as my husband."

"I would like to have a car. You could marry me, and then we could travel around together."

They were both amused and laughed at the thought of these ideas. Then a serious look crossed Star's face, and Jose asked about it.

"I'm beginning to believe that Jesus is the only way to God," Star said. "I believe He told the truth and we have to believe His Word. By that, I mean we have to agree with all that it says. When we do believe, our lives change and our actions show it. God changes us."

"You don't have to change," Jose assured her. "I love you the way you are."

"You don't know me very well. I have come to realize how selfish, critical, and jealous I am. I also want to do things my way all the time. I am quite proud of my Indian background and my looks. And I mean really proud! I used to consider other Indians to be below me and other people to be below them. But I have asked God to forgive me and take away all those bad thoughts."

"And has He done it?"

Star didn't answer the question. "You will know someday when you realize who God is."

Jose felt offended. "I'm not a bad person, and I haven't done any really bad things."

"Look at me," Star said. "I know you are good and honest and you wouldn't hurt anyone. I look well, and I don't feel sick. But I'm rotten on the inside. I was sick and I didn't know it." She had made her point with Jose.

He told her about the little church where they held Spanish services. "We'll go there together when you can leave for the day. I heard that some patients in the past have been allowed to work for wages outside and come back into the sanitarium to spend the night. I'll bet you will be well enough to leave by summer."

Star looked pensive for just a second. Then she smiled and shared Jose's optimism. She wondered what Dr. Watkins would say the next time they met. She also wondered if he would try to keep her here longer than necessary. She asked Jose if he could get her some more beads and sinew for beading. Her supplies were getting low, and she wanted to keep busy. She showed him exactly what she wanted and gave him money to take with him. Then she kissed her hand and placed it lightly on his cheek.

The following week, Star was surprised that she was asked if she would care to work in the office. The doctors approved of her helping out as long as she didn't overdo it. She was given the task of meeting visitors or people who came to inquire about getting into the sanitarium for treatment. She had a uniform that identified her as a non-patient. She worked four hours a day at first and continued to get plenty of rest and sleep. Her knowledge of Spanish made Spanish speakers more relaxed and less fearful of this new place. When a visitor came in looking worried about whether or not they would get well, Star could identify with them, and she would refer to herself as an example: "I have tuberculosis, and I'm getting well." Her appearance of robust health did much to help those who dreaded being there.

After Mary's operation and healing of her leg, she was asked to stay a month longer to be sure the disease was gone. She too was given a chance to work—in the food service division of the hospital. She was happy to have something to do, and her outlook changed radically. Mary talked as if she would soon be able to go home.

Shortly after the New Year began, Jose noticed some of the horses were not walking normally. They appeared dizzy and often stumbled. He advised Mr. Nelson, who called a veterinarian to look at the animals. The vet took samples of blood and sent them to a lab to be analyzed. They looked for a possible cause, and the vet read everything he could about horse diseases, but he could find little information to help him. Then he called the state university animal department and explained what was going on. They advised separating the sick horses from those that were showing no signs of having any problems.

Several days went by, and two horses died. Those horses that were taken to the ranch were looking good, and a few ponies in a small corral at the stables were all well—only the horses that Jose had the most contact with had been affected.

Finally, a report came back regarding the blood samples. There was some kind of poison found in the blood of the sick horses. That puzzled Mr. Nelson, and he asked Jose about the grain that had been given the horses. A few days before, Jose had opened a new sack of grain to feed the animals. Eight horses were sick, including the horses Mr. Nelson rode most and Jose's favorite horse. Mr. Nelson examined the grain and smelled it in the sack.

"It doesn't smell right," he said. "Don't give any more of this to the horses. We'll have to see if we can find out if someone purposefully poisoned this grain."

"Who would do such a thing?" Jose asked. "Who would harm such beautiful animals?" Jose's voice showed deep concern.

Mr. Nelson didn't tell him what he was thinking. He thought he had better wait until some evidence came in regarding possible culprits.

Finally, four other horses had to be destroyed. Jose became sadder than he had been since Wild Honey was shot. He thought long and hard about who might have had access to the grain, but he came up with nothing. He grieved over the loss of the horse he had ridden on trips through the mountains. It had been sure-footed and responded quickly to any situation.

Two days passed, and Mr. Nelson came up to Jose as he was working with the ponies. His face showed deep furrows, and he shared his thoughts with Jose.

"Don't tell anybody what I'm about to say. It would be premature. I have a competitor in this business, and he wants to see me quit. You know we make our money in the summer and losing six horses is a huge loss. People enjoy riding the same horse they are used to. I'll have to borrow some money to get some more good horses before the season starts. Keep an eye out for anything unusual and tell me, even if it turns out to be nothing."

"I'll be glad to sleep here at night if you want me to. The hay makes a good mattress."

Mr. Nelson laughed and said that it wouldn't be necessary. "But I want you to go with me when I look for some horses. It might take a couple of weeks, and there won't be many comforts. What do you say?"

"I think that would be fun. When do we start?"

"I'll let you know. By the way, I understand you spent some time at the hospital. Do you have family there?"

Jose's face lit up as he spoke of Star. "The girl I want to marry is there. She is recovering from tuberculosis. In a few more months, she should be well and able to leave. I live and work just to see her on Sundays."

Mr. Nelson's mind was on the trip he had to make. "When we find some horses, you may have to break them in to caravan over the mountains. We have got to have animals that are trustworthy and reliable on a narrow trail. As you know, some of those trails are pretty scary for city dwellers. I wouldn't want anyone to have an accident while riding."

Jose realized more of the responsibility that was involved. It caused him to become more careful and observant in his work.

When he visited Star the following Sunday, he told her the whole story of the horses and that he might have to be away for a few days. They were happy together, and they talked about marriage.

"It's hard to wait," Jose said.

"Just a little longer," she said softly.

Star's appointment with Dr. Watkins was scheduled for later in the week. A new X-ray was taken, and she waited patiently for the results. The doctor was talking with another female patient when Star arrived at his office. After a few minutes, the woman left. Dr. Watkins invited Star to come in, closed the door, and shuffled some brown envelopes on his desk. He took a negative out of one of the envelopes, and Star supposed it to be hers.

"Your X-ray shows that there is still some healing to be done. How do you feel? I see you are working four hours a day. I gave permission for you to do that."

"I feel fine and back to normal," she declared. "And now I am anxious to be able to spend days walking on the streets or riding out in the country or fishing in the mountain streams."

Looking at her sincere face, he responded, "I can arrange that. First, though, you must promise it will be with me."

Shocked by his request, Star replied in protest, "I will not!"

"And why not?" he challenged.

"You don't want to be seen with me. I'm a Kickapoo Indian."

"A what?" he almost shouted. "It makes no difference to me."

Star noticed some incongruity between his words and his body language. She wanted to break off the conversation but first had to level her last salvo at him.

"You—as a doctor—should not socialize with patients." She could see no change in his arrogant manner.

"I do as I like," he said in an angry and frustrated manner.

Star left the room with even less trust in her doctor. She wondered if there was a way she could talk with another doctor about the X-rays.

The chance came a day later when she was working in the office where the records were kept. She looked at her file, took out the latest X-ray, and took it to the hospital administrator. The man was sitting by his desk, and when he saw her, he invited her to come in.

"How can I help you?" he asked.

Star gave him the envelope and asked him to look at it and tell her what it meant. The man didn't question her motive or where she had gotten the X-ray. It was common for those coming in his office to carry their own X-rays. He looked at it carefully and faced her.

"It reveals some old scar tissue on one part of the left lung, but I see no reason to believe that there are fresh lesions anywhere," he told her.

"Thank you," she said with sincerity. "It makes me feel good because the X-ray is mine."

He smiled at her and wished her well.

Two days later, Star gathered together a few things that she had made. Then she inquired of her supervisor, "Would you mind if I take the day off? I will be going downtown, where the Indians gather to sell their wares and various arts and crafts."

After her supervisor gave her permission, Star left for downtown. There, she put her moccasins and ornaments on a cloth on the ground as the other Indians were doing. She sat down to wait for buyers. People came by, and she quickly sold most of her beadwork. She was happy that her things were selling quickly. All of a sudden, a voice came from behind her. She didn't have to look to tell whose it was.

"I finally found you!" he said with irritation in his voice. "You should not be here. You haven't been discharged from the hospital yet."

Star sat silently, not sure of what she should do. People were watching and listening to Dr. Watkins.

Not caring about the impression he was making, he continued. "Come with me and I will take you back. I have a buggy over there." He waited for Star to obey him. He thought she would get up and do as he had said. But he had no idea about what a tough woman Star could be.

"I won't ride with you," she said firmly.

"And why not?" he asked gruffly.

"I'm engaged to be married," she said. "I have a wonderful boyfriend, and I won't disappoint him."

"Jose is his name, right? He's a Mexican from South Texas, but he's just a goat herder," he said with obvious disgust. "He takes care of the stables and smells just like the horse barn." His voice rose, and he was becoming angrier every minute. "He shoes horses, and he will always be poor. You deserve more than that."

"Stop it!" Star ordered. "You insult him and me too. I love him, and I don't have to listen to any more of this. Get out of here!" She didn't waver from her position. The anger she felt was indescribable.

The doctor left with a final word. "You'll be sorry. This is not over."

Visibly shaken, Star walked back to the sanitarium. She knew the turmoil in her soul was not good for her physical well-being. At supper, she sat alone until Mary sat down beside her.

"Tell me about it," Mary said. "You look like a big tree collapsed on your tepee."

Star smiled at the image of a collapsed tepee, and she told Mary about the market incident.

"Whew!" Mary whispered. "He's got a real case for you. So he does know about Jose, but I wonder if even that will stop him."

"I don't know what to do," Star told her. "He talks like he can keep me here as long as he likes. I believe I am cured. In fact, I took my X-ray to the director, and he said he could see no more active spots on my lungs."

"How did you manage that?" Mary asked. "You could get into trouble if they find out about it. The files are private, and no one is supposed to look at them."

"It's my file, my record, and I have a right to see it," insisted Star. "I don't want to stay here one more day than I have to!"

The girls parted, and Star went to her room to rest. She was reminded of the sign posted in the hallway. In large letters it stated, "Total Rest=Body, Mind, and Spirit." She tried to achieve that, but disturbing memories still troubled her spirit. She opened her Bible to Psalm 23 and read it slowly and thoughtfully: "The Lord is my shepherd; I shall not be in want. He makes me lie down in green pastures; he leads me beside quiet waters. He restores my soul. He guides me in paths of righteousness for his name's sake. Even though I walk through the valley of the shadow of death, I will fear no evil, for you are with me; your rod and your staff, they comfort me. You prepare a table before me in the presence of my enemies. You anoint my head with oil; my cup overflows. Surely goodness and love will follow me all the days of my life, and I will dwell in the house of the Lord forever."

With deep gratitude for what she had learned since coming to the sanitarium, she prayed. "God, help me to trust you more." Then she slept for twelve hours.

When Star woke up, she found out she had slept through breakfast, but she wasn't hungry anyway. She put on her uniform, fixed her long black hair into a stack on the top of her head, and put a pretty beaded band around her forehead. Then she added a pair of turquoise earrings. She began her usual job in the office.

Nurses who came by told her she looked elegant, and some asked her who had done the beadwork. Wherever she went, her firm, straight figure commanded admiration and respect. That is, until Dr. Watkins saw her. He was speechless at first, but the anger in his heart left no room for admiration or praise.

"I want to see you in my office this afternoon," he said curtly as he moved away.

Star looked at the shadows on the ground outside the window and figured it was close to noontime. She went to her room and changed into her regular white dress and shoes. After lunch, she took a nap and did not wake up until about five o'clock. Remembering the doctor's words, she rushed to his office. He was obviously not pleased to see her at this late hour in the afternoon. He had only a few minutes left until appointment times would be over and he would be going home.

"Why are you so late?" he asked with irritation in his voice. "I asked you to come see me, and now my time is about up for today."

"I was tired and fell asleep," Star answered defensively. "What do you want?"

"I want our relationship to change," he said with much less hostility.

"What relationship?" Star said simply. She looked at him and made eye contact that demanded honesty.

Looking frustrated, he suddenly forgot his planned speech for Star. Her strong character disarmed him, but he clung to any little chance that she might have some place in her heart for him.

"I think of you constantly," he began. "I can't get you out of my mind, and I even dream of you. I think of ways to try to please you. I want you."

Star thought of a new tactic to take. "Do you know what people around here call you?" she asked. "They have given you the name of Tommy Hawk. They don't use the whole word. They just say, 'Tommy.' Now let me ask you, do you consider yourself a good doctor?"

"Why do you ask?"

"Do you remember the oath you took when you became a doctor?"

"What do you know about it?"

"Does it not say that you would always try to help the sick and preserve life?"

"Yes, in so many words, I guess it does. What are you driving at?"

Star wondered if she should mention the X-ray. She decided to do it. If it was wrong to have looked at it, she would admit it before he found out some other way to bother her.

"My X-ray shows that I am well. I feel well, and all the symptoms of tuberculosis are gone. I plan to leave here soon, and I'm grateful for the care you have given me." With that, she turned and started to walk out the door.

She heard him say, "Don't count on it," as she walked away.

She longed to see Jose and to tell him all about her feelings and stresses here. Jose would listen and understand what she had said. She prayed for the day when she could leave the sanitarium.

New patients arrived at the hospital, and other patients were discharged every day. One was Mary. She had recovered totally and now walked without a limp. Star's parting words to her were, "I want you to come to my wedding."

The joy and delight of leaving did not make up for all the sadness Mary felt about leaving Star.

"Come see me when you can," she pleaded. "I'll write to you when I get home."

Star kissed her forehead. "You are the closest person to a sister that I have ever had. Go with God." She gave her a pair of moccasins that had exquisite design, and the beads were brightly colored.

"They're beautiful." Mary was crying as she hugged Star tightly.

ACCEPTANCE

Jose was gone from town for a week. He and his boss located five good horses and started back home. Having a long way to go required them to sleep outdoors. They located a good place where the horses could eat their fill of grass and wouldn't wander. Mr. Nelson suggested that the two of them take turns staying awake just in case something came to scare the horses. Bears and timber wolves were plentiful in the area. The men made a fire and ate some beans, along with a pot of coffee, for supper. Jose slept first. Mr. Nelson awakened him around midnight. The horses were quiet, and the beautiful night sky, with a myriad assortment of stars, shed a faint light over the whole area.

Jose saddled his horse, knowing he would be less likely to go to sleep while sitting upright. Then he would be ready for any unexpected scenario. He moved a few yards from the fire that was still glowing. All of a sudden, the horses came alive with worry by snorting a warning. Jose's own horse—acting just like the others—wanted to move away. The animals had smelled a bear and were ready to run, reacting normally. First, though, they stood in a line like soldiers facing an enemy. They all faced in the direction of the bear. With their heads lifted high and their noses flared because of the bear's odor, they waited.

The bear must have smelled the food. Jose saw the big brute as it slowly and cautiously neared the camp. He knew that he had better awaken Mr. Nelson right away.

"Better get up," he told him. "There's a bear on the way."

Jose's boss got up and reached for the pistol at his side. The bear was sniffing the air and lumbering closer.

"Let's go down where the horses are," Mr. Nelson said as he mounted behind Jose. "We'll hope the old grizzly will leave us alone."

The bear licked the empty cans of beans and stood up to sniff the air. It was at least eight feet tall and could easily have killed a horse if provoked or if it became really hungry.

The horses had stopped eating and were all ready to run. They were watching and showing signs of nervousness. Jose didn't know if a horse could outrun a grown bear, but he didn't want to find out just now. Mr. Nelson whispered that they must stay quiet and wait to see what the bear did. The few minutes of waiting seemed like hours. Soon the bear left, and Jose put some wood on the fire. He knew that bears would stay away from a blazing fire. Mr. Nelson tried to go back to sleep, but it was useless. He knew the bear just might return and that they had to be on the lookout.

When daylight came, the party left and arrived at Mr. Nelson's stables by late afternoon. They were tired and hungry, so they put their horses in the corral, and both men fell on the piles of hay. Soon they were asleep.

The horses whinnied for hay or grain and awakened Jose. He moved among them while talking and patting their necks. Some horses were skittish about letting him touch their heads. He soon learned which ones would take the most work before letting clients ride them. He also found one of them to be quick to learn. Jose took it for his own personal horse to be used on long trips.

On June 1, the stables opened to the public. This was the day after school was out for the summer. It was a beautiful Saturday, and Jose was looking forward to seeing Star the next day. Some of the same students who had helped with the ponies before came again to help the children ride them. Jose told them all how much he appreciated their help.

Sunday morning found Jose at the service singing Spanish songs with the small group that met faithfully. A family invited him to dinner, and because he was so hungry, he accepted the invitation gladly. They lived in a modest house and had few earthly goods. But they were happy and showed unusual love for each other. One of the three children was retarded, but they all seemed to love him and showed unusual patience.

The family wanted to know about Jose, his background, and what he had done in Albuquerque. He gave them a quick account of his life and where he was working now. The children were spellbound when he told them that they could ride the ponies if they came to the stables while he was there.

"You won't even have to pay," he told them. "I will let you ride the best ponies if you come when I am there." Then he told them about Star, who had come to the sanitarium to get well. He said she was getting better and they planned to marry when she was discharged.

"Marry in our church," exclaimed the lady. "We'll decorate it for you, and it will be lovely."

"I would like that very much," Jose replied enthusiastically. "I'll mention it to Star this afternoon."

The man spoke up. "Star is such an unusual name for a woman. How did she get that name?"

"She's an Indian," replied Jose. "Actually, she is from Mexico and is the most beautiful woman in the world. You will agree when you see her."

One of the children spoke up. "Mommy is part Indian—Ah-wapa-hoe."

Everybody laughed. Jose showed them a small beaded pouch that Star had made for him. After the meal, he hurried to the sanitarium.

"I'm so glad you came," Star told him when he arrived. "I want to leave this place as soon as possible, and I believe I am well and should leave." She told him about the X-rays and also about the doctor who wanted to keep her here.

"Do you want me to punch him in the nose?" Jose said half jokingly. "Or would it be better if I just take him out to the wild country and leave him there for the grizzly bear to eat?"

Star laughed, and she realized that maybe Jose had encountered a bear. She asked him about it, and he told her about that night under the stars. He mentioned the wonderful family that had asked him to dinner that day. He was so excited about their offer to have him and Star marry in their church.

Star hated to put a damper on it, but she said, "I'm not out of here yet."

She thought that maybe this statement would close the door about further talk of marriage, but Jose, never tired of asking her, again said, "You will marry me, won't you?"

Star paused for a long moment, carefully thinking of how she should say it. "Jose," she began. "I must marry somebody who believes as I do, one who takes seriously the words of Jesus and calls him Lord. He has to love God more than me and be willing to do what He wants."

Jose became annoyed, and he showed it. "Let's not argue about what we believe. When we marry, you can go to any church you like and I'll respect your decision, but leave me with mine. It's enough that we love each other."

"Let me tell you how it is," she said softly and in a steady voice. "The Bible says a follower of Jesus should marry only one who is also a follower. It's like light and dark. They cannot exist together. This is what I'm praying for: that you will recognize your faults and sins, confess them to the Savior, ask for forgiveness, and become a Christian. I pray that you will be baptized with me as a testimony that we are new people. Then we can take communion together and be married."

She saw the huge disappointment in his face. Star felt that Jose was resisting something he knew to be true. He stood up to leave. As she had done many times, she kissed his hand and tenderly touched his cheek. She wished for his usual hug, but he said a quick good-bye and left.

Jose was miserable. However much he worked, the feeling wouldn't go away. In the evening he tried to read, but thoughts of what Star had said kept looming in his mind. The thought that she might not marry him was unbearable. He had waited and worked hard for that goal for a long time. The same uncertainty, unrest, and doubt that he had felt after Wild Honey was shot gripped him once again. He had to have some answers. More than once he thought of quitting his job, leaving Star, and moving far away.

For nearly a week, a battle raged within him. Turmoil and frustration prevented clear thinking. He made mistakes, injured one of his hands, and tolerated a great deal of pain because of his frustrations and misery.

Early Sunday morning, he went for a long walk into the mountains. Jose wanted to be alone, but he could not escape from the annoying feelings that had started after Star told him that they could not be married unless Jose believed as she did. His thoughts and emotions were like a pack of wild dogs harassing a wounded elk. His aimless walk took him far from the city. Time passed, but he felt no hunger. The sun was becoming lower in the sky, and he began the long trek home. He did not see Star that day.

After he returned, he noticed that the church door was open. Entering, he saw no one. Taking a seat in the front of the church, he looked up to the stained-glass windows. A shepherd held a small lamb in his arms. Jose immediately thought back to the many times that he had cuddled baby goats to his bosom and carried them home. He sat there for some time as he thought about the picture before him. Someone came in and greeted him.

"You have come to pray. Let's pray together," the man said.

"I don't know how to pray. I'm like that lamb in the picture up there. I am helpless and weak. I need help, and I don't know where to go," Jose confessed.

The man put an arm around Jose's shoulder. "Do you believe the Shepherd died for that lamb and that the lamb had nothing to offer nor money to pay for its life? You see, God forgives us when we come to him as we are. All our good works are worthless when it comes to being forgiven. Jesus paid all the cost for our freedom when He died on the cross, and His suffering and death will keep us from the sentence of eternal death if we will just accept Him as our Savior. He offers a free gift: Himself. He invites us to take him into our lives, and through Him we can live forever. It's called eternal life. Invite Jesus into your heart now. He is listening, and He will fill up that empty spot in your heart. You will be a new person. God will be your Father, and Jesus will be your best friend. There will be no record of wrongs that you have done."

The man waited. Time went by, and the silence became oppressive. A battle was going on in the spiritual realm that one could not see. Suddenly, Jose knew that this was what Pancho had said. Kayla's father said the same thing, and Ted had said it too. They all had what he lacked and really wanted.

"God," he began, "I don't know much about this, but I want Jesus in my life. Star has you, as does Ted. Pancho was also a son of yours before he died. Please wash all my sins away and make me new."

He was unaware that the man had left, and people had entered the church for evening prayers. He moved to the back and sat down. The room looked new to him. He sensed the presence of God, and he felt the freedom to really praise God for the first time. His heart was filled with song.

Meanwhile, Star had been in her usual place with others who gathered for worship in the sanitarium. All of them knew she was engaged to marry Jose, and they wondered how it would all work out. God had answered their prayers, and Star was well. She had stopped talking about marriage, however.

The next Sunday, Star and Jose shared some pleasant time together. She didn't press him about what they had talked about, and he remained cheerful and helpful.

"Do you suppose that you could go with me next Sunday to the church I go to?" he asked Star. "I want them to meet you. They're such great people."

Immediately, Star said, "Of course. I would love to go with you." She couldn't recall having been to a Spanish service. Upon leaving, Jose gave her a hard, meaningful hug.

During the week, Jose spent most of his spare time reading from the New Testament. He read it because he wanted to, and it spoke to him in new and wonderful ways. He wrote down things that he wanted to share with Star. When he prayed, he asked that God's will be done. When he worked with the new horses and got them used to the rails and new people, he asked for God's help.

Star's week went well also. The director of the hospital asked her if she would like to be a full-time staff member.

"Yes," she responded enthusiastically. "But I haven't been discharged yet."

"Really?" he said. "I'll take care of that."

He told her what her salary would be and that her work would be essentially the same as she had been doing. The news spread quickly throughout the hospital. When Mary came to visit, she gave Star a big hug and congratulations. She was given two weeks to find a place to live, and she didn't have to look long. One of the married women in the office offered her a room in her house.

Star and Jose went to the little Spanish church on Sunday. That day, Jose went forward after the sermon to accept Jesus Christ as his Lord and Savior publicly, and the church welcomed him into their fellowship. The church members all greeted him warmly, and Star was ecstatic that he had joined her in the faith. Everyone welcomed Star with open arms, and she felt right away that she belonged there. Her face showed pure joy when they sang the Spanish songs. She knew Kickapoo and English, but she felt Spanish was the language she knew best. The ladies lost no time in talking to her about how much they wanted the wedding to be in this church. One lady offered to provide the wedding dress, and some of the men offered to get a small band to play the music.

"We can talk some more about it next Sunday," she told everyone.

Star had asked many questions about weddings: what people did, what they wore, did they have a feast for the guests, and so on. Some of the staff at the hospital brought their wedding pictures for her to see.

"This is all new to me," she told them. "I have never seen a wedding like you describe. In my village, a couple goes to mass. The priest hears their vows, and then they go home. The two families and guests share a big feast with lots to eat. There's music and dancing for three or four days. The bride and groom dress in their usual work clothes.

A letter from Bluebird arrived the next day. Star was surprised because she hadn't heard from him for months. Quickly, she tore the letter open, and it contained short but wonderful news. Bluebird was coming to Santa Fe the last of June. Because she was excited and wanted to tell Jose as quickly as possible, she got directions to the stables. They were only two miles away, and it would be a pleasant walk for her.

When she got there, Star saw Jose talking to a man. Jose didn't see her, and she didn't call his name. He was telling the man about his newfound faith and the peace and joy he had experienced since inviting Jesus into his life. Star listened for a few minutes and found a box to sit on where she was out of sight. Then she reread Bluebird's letter. The man left the stables, and Jose started working on some broken straps. She called to him.

"Star!" Jose exclaimed loudly. "What brings you here?"

"I got a letter today from Bluebird, and he is coming soon. Isn't that wonderful?"

Jose broke out into a broad smile and was really happy that he would soon see his friend. He looked at the beautiful girl before him and longed to stay with her.

"First, I must ask Bluebird for your hand in marriage, Star. In our excitement, we almost forgot that I must do that. Let's plan our wedding while he is here," he suggested. "We'll marry in the church as the ladies have suggested, and it will be a wedding that honors God. We'll plan some more on Sunday, okay?"

Star's face beamed with joy. Jose looked serious and put his finger under her chin, raising it slightly. Searching her lovely eyes carefully, he hoped to find an answer there.

"Tell me," he implored. "With Bluebird's permission, will you consent to be my dear wife with whom I'll spend the rest of my life?"

"Of course I will. I love you," she declared without hesitation. "I'm so excited, and I am asking questions of people as to how to plan the wedding. I had better return before it gets dark." She looked at the sky. A huge white cloud covered it, and the sun's rays were bouncing off it like giant sparklers. She took it as God's confirmation of their plans.

"Let's ride together, and I'll come back later with the horse." Jose put her on a beautiful Palomino that was gentle and full of life. He saddled his own trusted mount. They took the long way to Star's house.

When Sunday arrived, the couple told their friends that Star's uncle would be coming, and plans for the wedding were made. She listened as some of their friends suggested various dates. That afternoon, Star and Jose talked about what they would do after the wedding. Should they stay in Albuquerque and work or go elsewhere?

Star spoke up. "We both have work, and we can save our money. First, we have to look for a place to live."

"You know what I'd like to do?" Jose said. "I would like to go back to Anadarko, where this all began. It has been about a year since we were there, and we can dream and plan as if we hadn't had this detour."

"That's an option," Star agreed. "But what would you do?"

"I'd like to follow the harvesting of the grain, just like I had wanted to do back then."

"Oh, let's wait and talk to Bluebird and see what his plans are."

They talked about how much the wedding would cost, and Jose told her he had two hundred dollars saved up, but he wondered if that would be enough.

She voiced a simple lesson she was learning. "We'll always have enough. God has promised to care for us."

They didn't know the exact date of Bluebird's arrival, but they decided on the date for the wedding. The whole staff at the hospital knew about it, and they gave Star a surprise party. The director of the hospital told her she should take her X-ray with her. He also told her that she should be sure she got her checkup every year, no matter where she went.

Bluebird arrived the very next day in a different car that was a bit newer than his old one. Star had dozens of questions about the people of her village. She was so excited that sentences tumbled over each other in Kickapoo and Spanish.

Jose spoke up. "Bluebird, will you give me your permission to marry Star? We have already started planning our wedding, so I hope you will say yes."

"Do I have a choice now?" said Bluebird. But Jose and Star could both tell that Bluebird was kidding them. "Jose, I know I could not ask for a better son-in-law than you."

"In that case," said Jose, "will you be my best man?"

"Of course. I will be happy to do so."

Star told Bluebird that the wedding would be in a Protestant church. He didn't question her decision.

Jose and Star met with the leaders of the church and asked to be baptized. They decided that the baptism would be on the Saturday before the wedding. A number of people gathered at a nearby river. The lay pastor explained what the sacrament of baptism meant. He said it was a public declaration of one's faith in Jesus Christ, as well as a commitment to be Jesus's disciple.

When the couple went down into the water, the leader dipped a pitcher of water from the river. As he poured the water on their heads, he said, "I baptize you in the name of God the Father; His Son, Jesus Christ; and the Holy Spirit."

Star's face glowed with joy as she realized anew that the two of them were united in a vital spiritual sense.

The church people decorated the trees in the churchyard with streamers, paper bells, and flowers. The colors of green, red, and white abounded in all of the decorations.

On Sunday, the service was cut short due to the wedding that was to follow. There were many guests from the sanitarium, and several of Jose's friends with whom he worked also attended the wedding. His boss and family came, showing their appreciation to Jose. The ceremony was simple and yet Christ-centered.

The final part was something that Jose and Star had rehearsed alone, and this was a surprise to the group. The two turned to each other, and Jose took Star's hand in his. She looked up with a radiant face, and he looked into her eyes as they said together, "Where you go, I will go, and where you stay, I will stay. Your people will be my people and your God, my God" (Ruth 1:16b, NIV).

The couple left the church, and they were greeted by lively mariachi players with their exciting music. Jose and Star sat down at a table in the place of honor and watched as helpers served food to everybody.

A friend of Jose's whispered in his ear, "I'll take you wherever you want to go after this is over."

Jose thanked him and then admitted, "I haven't even thought about that."

The man added, "How about ten miles away to a cabin in the mountains?"

A few of Star's best friends left some practical gifts for them—something that neither of them had expected. As things began to wind down and guests were leaving, Star and Jose thanked each for coming and for making the day such a memorable time.

Star and Jose spent their first night together alone, at a place far from the interruptions and cares of their lives.

They embraced passionately.

Star whispered in his ear. "Our love will never die."

"You are God's gift to me," Jose replied softly, "and I can think of no other blessing that can compare to you."